COCKY JERK

INTERNATIONAL BESTSELLING AUTHOR
JANINE INFANTE BOSCO

Cocky Jerk

© Copyright 2020 by Janine Infante Bosco and Cocky Hero Club, Inc.

All rights reserved. No part of this publication may be reproduced, distributed, or transmitted in any form or by any means, including photocopying, recording, or other electronic or mechanical methods, without the prior written permission of the publisher, except in the case of brief quotations embodied in critical reviews and certain other noncommercial uses permitted by copyright law.

This book is a work of fiction. All names, characters, locations, and incidents are products of the authors' imaginations. Any resemblance to actual persons, things, living or dead, locales, or events is entirely coincidental.

EDITOR: Virginia Tesi Carey

PROOFREADING by: Back2TheWall Edits

PHOTOGRAPHER: FuriousFotog

MODEL: Justin Michaels

INTERIOR FORMATTING & DESIGN: T.E. Black Designs; www. teblackdesigns.com

Cocky Jerk is a standalone story inspired by Vi Keeland and Penelope Ward's Stuck-Up Suit. It's published as part of the Cocky Hero Club world, a series of original works, written by various authors, and inspired by Keeland and Ward's *New York Times* bestselling series.

CHAPTER ONE

ANTONIA

MONDAY IS A MAN. DON'T try to argue with me, I am fully prepared to go to war on this one. Think about it, Monday comes too quickly…*way too quickly* if you get my drift. I mean, you're not even finished with Saturday and *bam*, Monday is already picking up its pants from the floor and asking if we can do this shit again next week.

Yeah, no thank you.

Sadly, though, you can't give Monday a phony number and write it off as a bad lover. All you can do is give Monday your middle finger and press on. Which is exactly what I did when my alarm clock failed to do its damn job. It wouldn't have been a big deal if today wasn't my first day as an intern for "Ask Ida," the infamous advice column that prides itself on aiding the misguided fools of New York City.

Can't get laid? *Ask Ida.*

Can't get your pet goat to walk on a leash? No problem, just *Ask Ida!*

Does your underwear keep riding up your ass? Have no fear, Ida's got you covered.

I couldn't wait to meet this Ida chick, seeing as I had a couple of questions for her myself. Questions like, how the hell do you get your overbearing father and his outlaw motorcycle club off your back and find a man who isn't intimidated by a girl who rides a Harley and swears like a sailor. I'd also like to know the winning lotto numbers and while I'm at it, who killed Jimmy Hoffa.

However, I wasn't going to be working for the elusive Ida Goldman, so if I wanted any of my questions answered, I'd likely have to submit them to the column along with the rest of the Tri-state area.

My job was with her assistant Soraya Venedetta and while Soraya seemed cool as fuck and totally my kind of people, I doubt she'd be keen on having an intern who couldn't get her ass to work on time. Especially on the first day.

So, I rolled out of bed, squeezed my ass into a pair of jeans and instead of my usual vintage rock band tee, I pulled a black thermal over my head. After all, I wanted to make a good impression. Lastly, I shrugged on my leather jacket and laced up my moto boots. My hair was a wild mess of curls, but there was nothing I could do about that except pray the helmet defrizzed the mane.

Ready to start my day, I made my way through the Corrupt Hellraiser compound. But there's no clean break when living with a bunch of bikers, though, and I was bombarded with questions.

Where are you going?
Who are you going to be with?
What do you mean you got a job?

By the time I threw my leg over my Harley, I had a half-hour to get from Brooklyn to Manhattan and unless my bike sprouted chrome wings, I was undoubtedly going to be late. I thought about sending Soraya a text, or maybe one of those edible fruit arrangements—something that said *Hey, I'm on my way. Have a strawberry and please don't fire me.* But I decided against both things, which I'm now regretting as I sit in bumper to bumper traffic on the Brooklyn Queens Expressway.

"Fuck this," I hiss, throttling my engine as I weave in between a tractor-trailer and an SUV. People say it's the early bird who gets the worm, but it's the aggressive driver who really makes shit happen. Twenty minutes later I'm exiting the Brooklyn Battery Tunnel like a boss, wearing a grin that's masked by my helmet. I might be running late, but I'm the envy of Uber drivers everywhere.

It's the little things, man.

The things that get squashed when you hear the distinct sound of sirens blaring behind you. I tell myself the universe isn't this cruel, that there is no fucking way I'm getting pulled over and I believe it so much so that I keep going—right through a red light. The sirens are soon paired with red and blue flashing lights, confirming I am indeed fucked, and the universe isn't just cruel, it fucking hates me.

Muttering a stream of curses that would make a street-walker blush, I veer my Harley over to the shoulder of the West Side Highway and drop the kickstand down. With an exasperated breath, I pull the helmet from my head, and shake out my wild curls. My gaze swings to the sideview mirror and I watch as the inconsiderate officer saunters over to me—it should be noted that this is all done at an incredibly slow pace like I'm not fucking late. Like there isn't someone, somewhere in this great big city who needs a crime-stopper. Rolling my eyes, I plant my boots on the ground and carefully balance my helmet between my thighs.

There are two ways I can play this shit. I can take the ticket like a champ, be on my merry way and pray I'm not fired before I punch the timecard, or I can attempt to wiggle my way out of it. I shouldn't really be considering the latter since I'm sure my hair looks like I stuck my finger in a socket, but I've lost count on how many points I currently have on my license. So, as the cop approaches, I throw my long locks over my shoulder and fix the girls. Luckily, in my haste of dressing, I grabbed a pushup bra.

Look who's winning now.

Planting a fake smile on my face, I turn my head and bat my eyelashes just as the cop steps next to my Harley. The smile falls from my lips and my eyes widen as I take in the hunky officer scowling at me. Standing tall and straight, the first thing I notice are his massive shoulders and his bulging biceps that fill his uniform. My gaze travels lower. His stance emphasizes the force of his thighs and the slimness of his hips where his belt sits holding his gun. It's an impressive package and I find myself lifting my head to check out his face.

While his eyes are hidden behind a pair of aviators, everything else looks delicious with a capital D. His wavy brown hair is perfectly styled and compliments his olive complexion. My gaze moves to his straight nose before settling on his full lips that, like everything else, are seemingly perfect. I'm sure a police officer never looked so fine.

Widening his stance, he crosses his arms against his chest and my eyes immediately dart from his lips to his corded forearms that are covered in vibrant ink and dusted with a sprinkling of dark hair. There's something about a guy's arms that just does it for me. In fact, I once dated a guy just because he had killer biceps. Everything else was a bust, but those arms…man, they were what dreams are made of.

"License and registration," he barks, startling me and forcing my focus back to his face. I swallow and remind myself that I need to get the hell to work, that there's no time to drool over a hunky cop. So what if he ticks off all my boxes. He's about to hand me my ass.

The thick gold chain around his neck and the gold horn that dangles from it, grabs my attention. Being Italian, I'm fully aware of the sentiment—well, I am now. As a kid, I thought my dad had a weird obsession with peppers, but it turns out the big burly biker known as Tank is superstitious and thinks the little gold pepper shaped pendant is going to ward off the evil spirits.

Suddenly, I feel a grin spread across my lips. Forget thrusting my double d's in this guy's face or batting my eyelashes at him, all I have to do is threaten the hunky cop with the malocchio and we can forget all about running the red light. He'll go pray to his peppers and I can get the hell to work.

However, before I can throw up my fingers and give him the evil eye he reaches up and pulls the aviators from his face, revealing a pair of soulful hazel eyes. Did I mention I'm also big on eyes? A flirty smile, big arms, killer eyes, and a fresh pair of Nikes are the way to my heart. He's yet to smile and in uniform, but two out of four isn't too bad.

"I said, license and registration." He basically growls as he tucks his glasses into his front pocket. My eyes dart to his badge and the little patch that reveals his last name.

Smiling, I lift my gaze back to those narrowed hazel eyes.

"I'm *so* sorry officer, Pirelli," I say, pointing a finger to the name embroidered to the patch as I bat my eyelashes. My wayward curls get caught in my lashes distracting me. I pause for a beat to push the hair away from my eyes before continuing, "You see I'm kind of in a bind. Today is my first day at my new job and I seem to have a case of the jitters…"

Who the fuck says the word jitters anymore?

"Anyway, I have this condition and I sort of lose feeling in my hands when I'm nervous." I don't even know what the fuck I'm saying at this point, but I hold up my hands and shake them to add extra emphasis to my fib.

Mr. Tall, Dark, and Handsome raises an eyebrow but doesn't say anything which leads me to continue with my ridiculous story.

"I squeezed too hard," I explain, offering him a mischievous smile.

"Sounds like a personal problem," he deadpans. "Or possibly carpal tunnel. You should probably go see a doctor…after you give me your license and registration."

The smile quickly vanishes from my lips as I become painfully aware he's not all that impressed with my antics. Huffing out a breath, I drag my fingers through my hair and tilt my head. Meeting his bemused gaze, I scowl miserably.

"You don't believe me, do you?"

He shakes his head unfazed.

"Not even a little."

Right, okay, well I tried.

Sighing, I lower my hands and search for my license. I pat down my leather jacket. Feeling the little card-holder thing where I store my I.D. and debit card, I pull out my license and hand it to him. He takes it and drops his eyes to my picture—which in case you were wondering is not the most flattering photo of me. While he studies my mug, I lift my ass off the seat and twist my body around to pop open my saddlebags. It takes me a good while to locate my damn registration card and when I finally turn around, I find Officer Pirelli checking out my ass.

Maybe there's hope after all.

Making it known I caught him staring at me I clear my throat. His gaze snaps back to mine and a sly grin spreads across my lips.

"My registration card," I singsong, waving it in front of him.

His jaw clenches and his eyes slightly narrow as he yanks the card from my fingers. "It's good to know all those squats I've been doing in the gym are paying off."

He opens his mouth to say something, but quickly smacks those full lips of his together. There's a certain intensity to him and it's hot as hell. If I wasn't so hell-bent on getting away from my father's club, I might be inclined to blow off my job at "Ask Ida" to play with the pepper worshipping cop. But I need this job. It's a paid internship and to lose it would only set claiming my independence from the Corrupt Hellraisers back a notch or ten.

"I'm going to need to see your insurance card too…" His tone trails as he reads my name from my license, "… Miss DeLuca."

My name rolls off his tongue with ease and my lips quirk. There's a smart remark sitting on the tip of my tongue, but it doesn't get past my lips. The teasing smile disappears from my face and I stare at him as if he's just asked me to recite the alphabet backward.

"My insurance card?"

Lifting his eyes from my I.D., he arches an eyebrow.

"Yeah, you know that little piece of paper that states you're insured."

Oh, for fuck's sake.

"I know what it is," I hiss.

He might be pretty, but he's clearly a dick.

"Well, then do you mind handing it over?"

I wouldn't mind at all if I had it on me, but my policy just renewed, and I forgot to print out the new cards. That's what happens when the whole fucking world goes paperless to save a bunch of trees. If you don't check your emails on the daily or forget the password to the gazillion accounts you have, you don't get your bills. Therefore, you don't pay them, and your credit score takes a nosedive. But never mind that, back to my insurance card situation.

Raising my head, I meet his expectant eyes and grimace.

"I don't have my insurance card on me," I confess.

"I see."

There's no chance in hell I'm getting out of this and I already wasted ten minutes of my life I'll never get back. Releasing an exasperated breath, I roll my eyes and look back at him.

"Can you just give me the damn ticket so I can be on my way?" I hiss the question and he smirks in response.

He. Fucking. Smirks. At. Me.

The balls on this guy.

Before I can properly react and tell him he's an asshole, he turns and he saunters back to his patrol car. Shamelessly, I watch his tight ass move in those dark blue pants. Then, I fold my middle and ring fingers down and lift the remaining three, giving him the malocchio.

Take that, you son of a bitch.

Turning back around, I continue to ogle him from my sideview mirror as he folds his large frame into the car and a sigh escapes my lips.

It's always the pretty ones that are the biggest jerks.

I glance at my watch and groan. I was supposed to be at the office an hour ago. Deciding to send the Edible Arrangement, after all, I grab my phone from the inside pocket of my leather jacket and start searching for a place that will deliver Soraya a bouquet of chocolate-covered strawberries. By the time I find one that isn't far from the office, the pain in the ass cop returns.

"Here's your license and registration," he says, offering them to me.

I pocket my phone and pluck my documentation from his fingers. That's when he extends his other hand and produces not one ticket, but *three*!

My eyes bulge as my temper flares and the license falls to the ground. I reach for the tickets and quickly flip through them. The first is for the light, the second is for failing to produce an insurance card, and the third is for speeding.

"You gave me a ticket for speeding?" I shriek, lifting my chin. His eyes meet mine, and he gives me a pointed look.

"You were going fifty-five in a forty zone."

Clenching my jaw, I glare at him. My blood pressure rises and my head pounds violently. If I wasn't sure the son of a bitch would arrest me on the spot, I would wrap my hands around his throat and try shaking some human decency into him.

"You're kidding me, right?" I shriek, waving the tickets in his face like a madwoman. "This is like six points."

"Actually, it's seven. Slow down Curly Sue and while you're at it, get that hand thing checked out. Squeezing too hard is definitely a problem."

He flashes me a grin, and of course, the sight is fucking spectacular.

What a damn shame.

Muttering a curse in Italian, I crumble the tickets into a ball and shove them hastily into my pocket.

"Have a nice day, Ms. DeLuca," he adds with a wink. Then he mumbles something, also in Italian and turns back to his vehicle. I'm about to lift my helmet back to my head when my gaze falls to the sideview mirror.

The bastard really does have a phenomenal ass.

As if he can sense I'm ogling his buns, he glances over his shoulder and I note he's still sporting that mischievous grin.

"You won't be grinning when your pepper fails you and your underwear rides up your ass all day, Pirelli," I mutter under my breath.

Fucking Monday.

CHAPTER TWO

ANTONIA

"CAN I HELP YOU?"

I arch an eyebrow as I stare at the receptionist—the same chick who brought me to meet Soraya last week when I interviewed for the position. Wondering if I look worse than I thought, I turn and glance at my reflection in the mirrored elevators. Ok, so my hair is much wilder than it was the day we met but other than that, I don't spot any significant changes. Turning back to her, I rest my helmet on top of the fancy counter that sits between us.

"We met last week," I remind her, forcing a smile. "I'm Antonia DeLuca, Soraya Vendetta's new intern—" she cuts me off.

"You're over an hour late."

"Well, yes, about that—"

"Penelope, I'm starting to get worried about my new intern. She was due into the office over an hour ago, can you give her a call to make sure—oh, there you are!"

Noticing me, Soraya steps out of her office. Her brows pinch together, and a look of concern washes over her features as she takes me in. When her eyes finally meet mine, she tucks a strand of her long straight hair behind her ear and I marvel over the royal blue ends. Not many people can pull off such a bold look, but Soraya nails it.

"You're late," she comments, crossing her arms over her chest. "I was beginning to think you decided not to take the position," she adds, clucking her tongue against the roof of her mouth. A flash of silver peeks out, and my eyes narrow curiously.

"Is that a tongue ring?" I blurt, instantly regretting the question when I hear Penelope gasp.

Alright, so maybe that's a little weird.

Feeling like a complete fool, I push a closed fist toward Soraya and try to make amends for the awkward question with a pound. "Kudos, girl. I pierced my tongue once as a big fuck you to my father. After twelve hours of drooling and not being able to talk, I ripped the thing out."

Shit.

Realizing I just dropped the f-bomb, I drop my fist to my side and raise my other hand, smacking my open palm to my forehead.

"I'm sorry," I mumble. "This has been the worst day ever," I continue, peeling my hand away from my face. "My alarm clock didn't go off as planned and then there was traffic, and this annoying cop who decided to make his monthly quota of tickets with me." I reach into my leather jacket and pull out the ball of tickets as proof. "I sent you an edible fruit arrangement, did it arrive?"

"You sent me an edible arrangement?"

I nod.

"Strawberries, pineapple…all that jazz." She stares at me blankly, and I swear Penelope mutters something that sounds oddly like *kiss ass*. Ignoring the receptionist, I continue, "Look, I really need this job. I swear if you give me a shot, you won't regret it."

It's true, while I have no experience in this field or any field really, I'm prepared to work my ass off. Waiting for her to respond, I nervously close my hand around the ball of crumpled tickets.

Please don't fire me.

Can you fire someone who hasn't actually worked yet?

"Traffic is ridiculous at this time," she finally says. "Where are you coming from?"

"Brooklyn."

A small smile ticks the corners of her bright red lips.

"That's where I'm from. Well, originally…" Her smile widens as she subconsciously thumbs the impressive rock on her left ring finger. "Now I live on the Upper West Side with my husband, Graham, and our two kids, Chloe and Lorenzo."

"So, there's hope," I say.

She laughs.

"There's always hope, girl," she replies, pushing off the doorjamb. Her eyes move to Penelope. "Penelope, I'm going to show Antonia to her desk. Can you bring her the new hire forms and make sure she's properly set up with an email account to field column questions?"

"Wait, so, I'm not fired?"

"Not today," she says cheekily. "Come, I'll show you to your desk."

For the first time since I opened my eyes this morning, I breathe a sigh of relief. Maybe Soraya is right, maybe there's hope to be found in every situation, even the ones that seem hopeless. She turns and starts for the row of cubicles, bypassing the office she appeared from. Penelope gives me a dirty look, but I don't acknowledge it or her for that matter as I shove the ball of tickets back in my pocket and grab my helmet from the reception desk. This day just turned around and nothing is going to bring me down.

I follow Soraya, watching as her pin-straight hair sways with every step she takes. I'm curious to know if there is a specific reason as to why she dyes the ends blue and why just the ends, why not the whole head—I mean if anyone can pull it off, I'm sure it's her. However, I don't ask.

Soraya sets me up in the cubicle closest to her office, which used to be hers, and reveals the reason I was hired. Apparently, the famed advice columnist, Ida, has decided to semi-retire. In the wake of the announcement, Soraya was promoted, and they needed someone to filter through the submissions for the column.

Enter me, the new filterer.

However, I can't start reading through the cries for help until I fill out the necessary new hire paperwork and Penelope sets me up with email access. Until then, I'm to organize the mess Soraya has left behind…and by mess, I mean there is shit everywhere. I can barely see the desk through the stacks of paper and the tower of paperclips that oddly resembles a miniature replica of the Empire State Building. Then there's the Post-its that wallpaper the cubicle. Some have little quotes, others have doodles, but the majority of them are responses to submissions and full of expletives.

I think I'm going to fit in just fine here.

"Any questions?" Soraya asks, drawing my attention back to her.

"What should I do with all these papers and Post-its?"

"Papers can be filed in the cabinet next to the window. As for the Post-its—well, there's some great material there…" her voice trails as a sense of nostalgia washes over her features. "Keep them," she decides, tearing her eyes from the colorful squares. "I have an appointment at noon, and my inbox is overflowing with emails I need to get through, but if you have any questions just holler."

"Will do."

She winks at me before turning and heading for her office, but before she goes, I feel compelled to thank her again for not firing me on the spot.

"Soraya?" I call. She stops midstride and glances over her shoulder at me. "Thanks for giving me a shot. I promise I won't be late tomorrow."

A warm smile spreads across her lips.

"It's all good. I'm a firm believer in second chances.

Yeah, I'm totally a fan of my new boss.

I SPENT THE FIRST HOUR organizing the paperclips and rearranging the Post-its. My cell phone pinged the entire time with calls and texts—all from my father, and all of which I ignored. By this time, I figured the guys had filled him in on my new job and he was likely freaking out. God forbid the princess of the Corrupt Hellraisers does anything without an entourage of bikers following her. I felt guilty for hiding my job from my dad, but I knew that's exactly what would have happened if I had clued him in. Ruger or Ritmo would be planted outside the office, trying to get a blow job from Penelope, and I'd be toast.

Silencing my phone, I shove it in the top drawer of my desk and glance at the stack of papers still waiting to be filed. I probably should've tackled that mess before the paperclips. My attention is drawn away from the dreaded task as Penelope clears her throat. I lift my head as she shoves a folder and an iPad in my direction.

"I see you're hard at work," she sneers, sarcastically.

This one is going to be a problem—I can just feel it.

"If you wouldn't mind putting down the paperclips, we can get you into the system," she continues, dropping the folder and iPad on top of my desk. "You'll need to fill out these forms for payroll and I'm going to need to make a copy of your driver's license."

The ringing phone interrupts her tirade and she turns to answer it, leaving me with the paperwork. I briefly thumb through the pages before reaching into my jacket for my I.D. My hand closes around the ball of tickets and I throw them on the table. Instead of reaching back into my pocket for my license, I let my gaze linger on the tickets for a moment.

Being a glutton for punishment, my treacherous mind wanders back to the hunky cop with the killer arms. It's a real shame he was such an asshole. I mean, a clean-cut guy with arms like his. His ass was nothing to sneeze at either and let me not forget those expressive eyes and slicked back hair. He had so much going for him. I could probably even get over his beliefs in ridiculous Italian superstitions, but his profession was a big red flag. Cops and I don't jive, mainly because of my father and while I'm ready to break ties from the Corrupt Hellraisers, I'm not looking to stick it to my old man for a quick roll in the hay with a man who carries a badge.

That's a hard pass.

Pushing all thoughts of Officer Pirelli to the back of my head, I pull out my I.D. case, only to discover my driver's license is missing. Figuring I must've shoved it into one of my pockets in a haste to get to work, I pat them down. Penelope reemerges and rolls her eyes dramatically.

"Are you kidding me? You didn't even touch the forms."

"I can't find my license," I hiss, slightly panicking. I

dump the contents of my pockets onto the desk and filter through everything. "Maybe it's in one of my saddlebags," I say, more to myself than to Penelope.

"Is that a designer? Like Gucci or Dior."

I lift my head and my jaw goes slack as I stare at her in disbelief.

She can't be serious.

Before I can explain what the fuck a saddlebag is or even decide if I want to entertain her with a response at all, the phone rings again at the reception desk and the handbag connoisseur rushes to answer it. I take off toward the elevators. Reaching them, I punch the button and glance over my shoulder at Penelope.

"If Soraya asks, I went to the parking garage to see about my license," I tell her, but she dismisses me with a wave and continues with her phone conversation. I stare at her for a beat, still trying to process the fact she thought a saddlebag was a designer handbag.

The elevator dings behind me, signaling the doors are about to open and I tear my eyes away from the clueless receptionist. Spinning around, I collide with something hard. Strong hands grip my waist, steadying me, and I lift my chin to apologize to whoever I've just barreled into. However, the words die on my tongue as I stare up at Mr. Tall, Dark, & Handsome, also known as the hunky cop. That hard thing I bumped into—that would be his chest.

"You've got to be shitting me," I hiss in disbelief.

What the fuck are the odds?

CHAPTER THREE

MARCO

"**Y**OU!" THE SEXY AS FUCK brunette shrieks as she pokes a finger against my chest. For a split second her eyes flit to where she touches me and a look of shock wears on her pretty features. It's fleeting though, because in a flash those brown eyes come back to mine and a scowl finds her face.

Antonia DeLuca.

I don't usually make a habit of remembering the names of every bad driver I pull over, but this one left an impression. I don't know if it's the eyes that drew me in or her full lips that seem to always be frowning. Maybe it's the mane of wild curls that I've spent the better part of my morning wondering what they'd feel like wrapped around my fist as I bend her over her bike—which, by the way, is a work of art. It's a goddamn shame she doesn't know how the fuck to drive it.

It isn't until she shoves my hands away hastily that I

realize I'm still firmly gripping her hips. She lifts her chin and glares at me with fury.

Fuck that's hot too.

"What are you doing here? Are you following me?" she snaps, narrowing her chocolate-colored eyes into tiny, narrow slits.

"Following you?" I scoff, unable to hide the smirk. Curly Sue may be nice to look at, and I'm guessing by the steam rolling off her, she's probably a real good time in the sack too. The high-strung ones usually are. It's all that anger and bad energy, it makes for fantastic sex. But the day I follow any woman around is the day my dick falls off.

"I know your kind," she sneers, pointing a finger at me again. This time she's careful to avoid touching me. "You think that badge makes you high and mighty, but I have no problem filing harassment charges against you."

Being a cop wasn't my first pick when it came to choosing a career—hell, it wasn't even my second. I used to bitch about my mother to anyone who would listen. See, growing up, she was strict, and her favorite pastime seemed to be busting my balls. At fourteen she made me get a paper route and sick and all, she made sure I delivered those newspapers every Sunday. Carmella Pirelli wasn't raising no bum. She was an old school Italian American woman, and if it wasn't for her insisting I take every city test, I'd likely be sleeping until four in the afternoon on her couch that she still keeps covered in plastic.

I paid the registration fees and took the tests for the police department, the fire department—even sanitation— all just to shut her up. It wasn't until I lost my job in construction that I finally had an appreciation for my ma's efforts. The academy called me five days after I cashed my last unemployment check, and I learned a valuable lesson.

Life doesn't always go according to plan. Take the fucking insurance policy.

The NYPD was my insurance policy and so, yeah, being a cop wasn't a lifelong dream of mine, but it's still very much a part of who I am. I bleed blue and I take offense to Curly Sue insinuating I use my badge for any reason other than to protect the citizens of New York. Alright, so I may have picked up a girl or two by telling them I had a pair of handcuffs in my back pocket, but for the most part, I'm all about catching the bad guys and of course, the occasional reckless driver.

"Is that what you cops do? Pull women over, get their credentials and stalk them at their place of employment after handing them a stack of tickets? There's gotta be a better way for you to get laid. Another method, perhaps. You know, one a little less creepy and that doesn't make you come off as a giant asshole."

Hot with a dash crazy—just how I like 'em.

"Wait a minute, let me get this straight. You think I pulled you over to get you in my bed?" I ask, mildly amused.

"I saw you checking out my ass," she accuses.

Ok, so maybe I was checking her out. I mean, her ass is spectacular, but there's no way in hell I'm fucking admitting that to her. Her head is already the size of Mount Rushmore.

"I was checking to see if your taillight was busted. In case you were wondering, it is, and I could've given you another ticket, but you seemed like you were having a bad morning, so I spared you. A thank you would be nice," I say pointedly as I cross my arms against my chest.

Her eyes go as wide as saucers, and she starts cursing in Italian. There's a *vaffanculo* in there and a *pezzo di merda* too.

Basically, she tells me to fuck off and calls me a piece of shit and somehow, I find that hot as fuck— go figure.

"Let's get something straight. My morning was going just fine until you pulled me over. Not only did you make me late for work, you gave me three tickets, *three*, and because of you, I lost my license!"

I roll my eyes. Great, so Curley Sue likes to exaggerate.

"You won't lose your license if you take one of those defensive driving courses, which is probably a fantastic idea considering you can't drive for shit."

"My physical license!" she shouts, gritting her teeth. "You know the little card with my picture, address, and date of birth that proves I'm a fucking resident of New York!"

Frustrated, she lifts her hand and threads her fingers through her hair just as she did when I pulled over. I was jealous of her fingers then and just as jealous now.

I uncross my arms and scratch my temple. I specifically remember handing her back her license, then she dropped it and I don't recall either of us bending to pick it up. I'd remember that ass perched high in the air for sure. However, before I can reveal any of that to her, the reason I'm here clears her throat. I tear my eyes away from the fiery woman in front of me and stare at the one standing behind her.

Her big brown eyes bounce from Antonia to me as my gaze zooms in on the ends of her hair, noting they're blue— a sign that all is well in the land of Soraya. If they were red or even purple, I would've turned the fuck around and got the hell out of dodge. One crazy Italian broad is enough for today, no need to be an overachiever.

"What's going on here?" Soraya questions.

"I'll tell you what's going on," Antonia hisses. "This asshole is the reason I was late this morning and now he's stalking me."

Suppressing a smirk, Soraya looks at me.

"On top of that, he stole my license!"

And there's the giant red flag. A total no-fly zone.

"For fuck's sake," I growl. "I didn't steal your goddamn license and quit accusing me of stalking you. I'm not here for you, something you'd know if you let me get a word in edgewise."

She crosses her arms and rolls her eyes, keeping them pinned on Soraya.

"Right, and I'm an astronaut."

"God, I hope not," I mumble. "You can't drive a motorcycle; I'd hate to imagine you manning the controls of a rocket ship."

"Marco, stop," Soraya chastises, but there's a hint of humor in her tone.

"Wait. *Marco?* You know this clown?"

Soraya chuckles.

"I do," she confirms. "He's my twelve o'clock." She glances back at me. "Did you really pull her over and give her three tickets?"

"I could've given her four."

She cocks her head and tosses me an exasperated look before focusing back on Antonia. With a sigh, she says, "Listen, today hasn't been the best and we can't put you in the system without your license, so why don't you go home, and we'll try this again tomorrow."

The anger fades from Antonia's face as she stares at Soraya apprehensively. It's a different look for the wild woman and dare I say, a little endearing.

"Is that your polite way of firing me?"

Soraya laughs.

"If I was firing you, you'd know it." She points both thumbs toward her chest. "Queen of second chances, remember?"

Antonia doesn't look all that convinced and for some reason I feel compelled to intervene.

"Yeah, this one doesn't hold back. If she wanted you gone, she'd have me escort your ass out of the building."

As soon as the words leave my lips, I realize I should've kept my mouth shut because this crazy girl hates me and when she turns to glare at me, she proves just that.

"I'd like to see you try."

Suppressing a grin, I shrug my shoulders.

I'm game if she is.

"Might be fun."

"Marco, leave her alone," Soraya reprimands, but it's hard to take her seriously when she's trying not to chuckle. Turning back to Antonia, she assures her that her job will still be there tomorrow and tells her to take the rest of the day to figure out her license situation. Antonia reluctantly disappears toward her cubical to grab her belongings as I toy with the idea of going back to where I pulled her over to see if her license is still in the street.

Feeling Soraya's gaze on me, I push the wayward idea to the back of my head and focus on my longtime friend.

"What?" I question.

Smirking, she shakes her head.

"Nothing. Let's go, I'm starving," she says, taking my hand as she drags me toward the elevator and stabs the button with her finger.

"Your husband knows about our little lunch date, right? He's not going to magically appear at the restaurant and bust my face open with a right hook, again, is he?"

Yeah, that happened.

Once upon a time, Soraya called on me to make her now husband jealous. Ever the helpful friend, I volunteered my services and posed as the new guy in her life. I suppose our mission succeeded since the pretty boy dislocated my jaw. But, hey, I'm trying to let bygones be bygones. I even shook the guy's hand and gave them a fat envelope at their wedding.

I'm all for being the bigger man.

WE GO TO KATZ DELI for lunch. They have the best pastrami in all of New York City and that's not a matter of opinion, it's a damn fact. I'll fight anyone who says otherwise. I'm halfway finished with my sandwich when Soraya whips out a notebook and pulls a pen from her cleavage. Completely unfazed by her ways, I take another bite as she goes over her checklist.

About a month ago she called me, asking to meet up for lunch. Soraya's best friends and my cousins, Tig and Delia, are celebrating their tenth wedding anniversary in a couple of weeks and since they've been having a rough time lately, Soraya thought a surprise party would lift their spirits. Tig is a giant pain in my ass, but him and Delia are family and when family hurts, I hurt. Besides, I'm all for a good party. We met two days later and have been communicating through text daily. It's the most we've spoken since she got hitched, and I realize I kinda miss having her as a constant in my life. So what if her husband is a stuck-up suit, Soraya is good people and you can never surround yourself with too much of that, especially when there are so many assholes in this world.

"Are you listening to me?" she asks as the wrapper of her straw hits my forehead.

I have no fucking idea what she said, but I nod with my mouthful of pastrami and reach across the table to snatch the lonely pickle on her plate. It's a sin to waste food.

"So, what do you suggest we do?" she presses.

Fuck.

"About what?" I reply, forcing the pastrami down my throat. She sighs exasperatedly and flips her Pocahontas like hair over her shoulder.

"You weren't listening!"

"I'm sorry, repeat it one more time, dollface," I say, grinning at her sheepishly. It's a piss-poor consolation prize for not paying attention to her. The last thing anyone needs is for those blue tips to turn red. Graham will have my ass, I'll be stuck planning this party by myself and everything will turn to shit.

"You need to figure out a way to get Tig and Delia to the party."

"Whoa," I say, nearly choking. "Why are we giving me the hardest job?" Tig and Delia own a tattoo shop on Eighth Avenue and unless there is an apocalypse there is no way in Hell they're going to shut down their shop on my account.

"Someone has to do it."

"And we think that someone should be me?"

"Why not? You're going to have to connive a way to get them both out of working. It's a miracle they showed to my wedding, and that was just a small thing in City Hall." She pauses to frown. "If you had a girlfriend, this would be easier."

How does me not having a girlfriend relate to any of this?

"Excuse me?" I question.

"We could tell them you were proposing or something. They wouldn't miss that for anything."

She's right.

Because they'd have to see me down on one knee to believe it was happening.

Like Antonia is a no-fly zone, so is fucking marriage.

"Right, okay, so marriage and a girlfriend are not an option," I tell her.

I can't believe I have to even say that out loud.

Crazy, I tell you. The whole fucking female species is absolutely nuts.

"That's a shame," she volleys, taking a massive bite of her sandwich. "I saw you checking out my new intern and…" her voice trails as she chews. "…don't try to deny it or spin me some bullshit story like you did with her. Checking out her tailpipe? Really, Marco? Is that the best you could come up with?"

I thought that was pretty creative.

"And did you really pull her over and give her all those tickets?"

I stare at her blankly.

Is she kidding me with that question?

"You make it sound like I did something wrong."

She shrugs her shoulders.

"I mean, you didn't *have* to give her three tickets. Hell, you didn't have to give her any at all, you could've let her go with a warning. Especially if you're attracted to her."

"It's my job to give tickets."

She rolls her eyes and takes another bite of her sandwich.

"You're a cop Marco, not a fucking meter maid, and Tig told me a story where you pulled over three girls in one day and got all their numbers."

"It was one time, and I was fresh out of the academy," I argue, silently cursing my cousin.

He's worse than a gossiping woman.

"So, you didn't pull over my intern because she's smoking hot?"

When did the conversation go from planning a surprise party to me picking up chicks? I need to start paying more attention to people when they talk and stop robbing food from their plates when they're not looking. Then I can avoid ridiculous conversations like this one.

"You know what I think."

Christ, please make it stop.

"Maybe you did pull her over because she disobeyed some traffic regulation, but once you got a dose of her, you wanted more. Let's be real, Marco, you like them hot and feisty. You wanted to see if you could get a rise out of her, so you gave her three tickets. But you dropped the ball. Instead of getting her digits and a date for Friday, you're the one who got a rise. Am I right?"

And this is why we stopped talking on the regular even before she got herself a husband. Soraya has no fucking filter and no problem sticking her nose in other people's business.

"You're out of your mind," I scoff, shoving another pickle into my mouth. "She sped right through a red light. Hot or not, I would've pulled anyone who did that over."

"Ahah! So you admit she's hot."

"Well, I'm not denying it," I say, crunching down on the pickle. "Why the hell do you have an intern, anyway?"

"Ida has taken a lighter load, so now that I have more responsibilities, Antonia is the one who will be filtering through the submissions."

I ponder that, trying to picture the Harley riding hottie behind a computer screen from nine to five.

"She doesn't seem like the type for office work," I comment.

"You know her five minutes."

That may be true, but I'm a good judge of character and confining that woman to a cubicle for eight hours a day would be as successful as trying to baptize a cat.

"Shit," Soraya says, glancing down at her phone. "I have to go. Graham is tied up at the office and I have to get Chloe from school."

She reaches into her bag for her wallet and I stretch my arm across the table, gripping her wrist.

"Get out of here," I tell her. "I got lunch."

We go back and forth for a moment and she offers to leave the tip. When I finally convince her to put her goddamn money away, she hitches her purse over her shoulder and tosses me a saucy grin, advising me to make nice with her new intern the next time I drop in for a party planning session.

She's barely out the door when my phone dings with a text.

Soraya: You should send her one of those edible fruit arrangements. I hear she's a fan. Oh, and don't forget to figure out a way to get Tig and Delia to the party.

There's no use in arguing with Soraya and so I don't bother with a reply. Instead, I order myself another pastrami sandwich to go, pay the bill and drag my ass out the door. Before I start my journey back to Brooklyn, I make a pit stop to where I pulled Antonia over. I decide if I find her license in the street, it's a sign to make nice with the fiery intern. If it isn't there, well, then I guess I'll push her out of my head, like all the others.

It's a good plan.

A solid one.

So tell me how come I don't follow it.

CHAPTER FOUR

STALKING THROUGH THE CLUBHOUSE, I slam my helmet down on top of the wooden bar. My eyes connect with the man standing behind it and a groan erupts from the back of my throat. How do you make a horrible day worse? Throw the guy you once thought you loved into the mix.

Sergio, more commonly known around these parts as Hound, turns around from the fully stocked shelves behind the bar and meets my gaze. Raising a pierced eyebrow, he drinks me in. There used to be a time when the way he looked at me excited me and made me feel wanted. Then I realized I wasn't special, that he looked at everyone with a pair of tits and a vagina the same way—hence his road name.

"Well, well, if it isn't the princess," Hound taunts playfully. A frown ticks the corner of my lips as I continue to stare at him. It's a shame he's such a jerk because he's a Rockstar in bed and he's not all that bad to look at. He's a lot more rugged than the hunky cop, and his eyes aren't nearly as intoxicating—Christ.

Did I just admit to myself that I find a cop's eyes intoxicating?

What the fuck is wrong with me?

Shaking my head, I divert my attention away from my ex-bedmate and step behind the bar.

"Fuck off, Hound, I'm not in the mood," I sneer, plucking a bottle of tequila from the shelf.

"Hey, I didn't log that, yet," he says, trying to snatch it from my hands.

Ignoring him, I move the bottle out of his reach and unscrew the top. I don't waste time reaching for a glass and bring the bottle to my lips, taking a long swig. I welcome the burn that spreads down my throat and warms my chest. A couple more shots and maybe I can forget all about this day.

"Whoa," Hound says. "You might want to go easy on that, Princess. That's the hard shit. But you like it hard, don't you?"

Such a jerk.

Lowering the bottle from my lips, I wipe my mouth with the back of my hand and roll my eyes.

"You know what I hate more than someone telling me what I should and should not do? Having someone call me princess. I fucking loathe that."

"Everyone here has been calling you princess since you were in your mother's womb," he says. "Now, it's suddenly a problem?"

Nope, it's been a problem for years, but no one wants to acknowledge it. They say I'm spoiled and call me a bitch. To everyone with a patch, I'm an ungrateful pain in the ass they're stuck protecting.

Tank DeLuca's princess.

Untouchable.

Unfuckable.

Unlovable.

One and three only applied to Hound. He had no problem fucking me just so long as my dad didn't find out. Heaven forbid his patch be in jeopardy because of little old me.

Taking another pull from the bottle, I set it down and meet Hound's gaze.

"Where's Mouse?" I ask, already losing my patience with him.

"What do you want with Mouse?" he volleys, removing the bottle from my reach. I don't argue with him. Instead, I watch as he scribbles a check on the clipboard and returns the tequila to the shelf where I snatched it from.

Mouse is the tech guy, the only one of the Corrupt Hell-raisers with a talent for something useful. He can give you a new identity and a million dollars in an offshore account, all with the flick of his wrist. This also means he can whip up a copy of my license and I can try this intern shit again tomorrow without any hiccups.

I don't owe Hound any explanations, though.

"Why don't you just tell me where he is?"

He considers my question for a second before placing the clipboard on the bar and crossing his arms against his chest.

"You know your father is looking for you," he counters. "Nearly blew his fucking lid when I told him you were starting your new job today." He pauses to uncross his arms and braces both hands on the edge of the bar. Leaning forward, his gaze drops to my mouth for a split second a familiar pull tugs at me.

Maybe he's not the jerk after all.

Maybe it's me.

I'm the jerk.

The jerk who still wants him because she's lonely and miserable.

"Why didn't you tell him you got the internship?"

The bad thing about kicking Hound out of my bed and severing ties with his dick is that I also lost my only confidant here. Being Tank's daughter is a lonely job and sometimes after we were done having sex, I'd talk to him about what was going on in my life. The things I wanted to achieve and the things I hoped to see. I don't think he paid much attention, but he laid there quietly and didn't interrupt me. I don't miss him, but I miss that.

Maybe that's why I engage.

"So he could talk me out of it?" I say with a sigh.

Hound shakes his head. His face grows rigid as he angrily narrows his eyes on me.

"You ever think there's a reason he might do that? That it isn't safe for you to be parading around without security? For fuck's sake why do you think he moved you into the compound?" he fumes.

Anger floods me and before I can think better of it, I grip the edge of the bar and match his stance.

"I don't know why he moved me into the compound because my father doesn't tell me shit. He orders me around like I'm some little puppet…like I'm a possession. And you all treat me the same. It's like the Corrupt Hellraisers own me."

He inches even closer to me and his eyes flicker with something I can't quite place, but my position doesn't falter. If you've seen one menace, you've seen them all and when your father is the king, not much scares you.

"Newsflash, Princess, we do own you and the fact that you are constantly being reckless is another problem this club don't need. Not when things are—"

"Hound!" my father bellows from behind me. "That's enough."

Hound's jaw ticks with annoyance as his gaze flits over my shoulder. Without another word, he backs away from the bar and holds his hands up as if he's surrendering.

"She's all yours, Prez. Good luck."

"What the fuck is that supposed to mean?" I challenge.

"Antonia," my father snaps. His Brooklyn accent sounds heavier than usual. "Backroom. Now," he orders roughly.

Great.

If I go back there, I know what's going to happen. He's going to tell me to quit my job or find some sort of way to control me. It's what he does. He doesn't mean any harm; he just doesn't know any other way. When chaos and mayhem are the banes of your existence, you can't help yourself. You try to control the little that you can. Like your daughter. But I'm done being controlled. It's not about defying my dad; it's about becoming my own person. Maybe this job at "Ask Ida" isn't where I'm supposed to end up. I mean, let's be real if I make it a week it'll be a miracle. But it's a step in the right direction. A step away from this place.

Unwilling to meet my father's gaze, I push away from the bar and keep my back to him.

"No," I argue.

Hound mutters a curse, but I don't give him the satisfaction of acknowledging him. Blowing out a ragged breath, I tuck my hair behind my ears and take a step toward the door.

"Antonia, where the hell do you think you're going?" my father barks. "I said—"

I pause mid stride and finally turn to face him. His dark brown eyes soften instantly and for a minute, I'm not a woman asking her dad to let her go. For one single minute,

I'm his little girl. The little girl whose hair he'd braid when all the kids at school made fun of her wild curls.

"Tonia," he murmurs on a sigh, scrubbing a hand over his face.

I don't know how many times we're going to have the same conversation. I wish someone would just tell me what it's going to take, what I'm going to have to say to get him to understand. I love him, but I hate what he stands for and I'm so tired of feeling like I'm stuck.

Swallowing, I force myself to look him in the eye.

"This is your life, your choice and no one can take that from you. All I want is a chance to choose a life that I love too."

He doesn't respond, but that's nothing new.

"Going home," I say, pausing to swallow the boulder clogging my throat. "Home, Dad, where all our pictures are, and Grandma's china sits in the cabinet untouched."

Home, where corruption and chaos don't live.

"Please don't follow me."

I probably shouldn't have stormed out of the club-house until I persuaded Mouse to hook me up with a license, but no, I had to go all girl and get emotional without pinning the tech guy to the wall. Something I realize as soon as I pull my Harley into the driveway and drop down my kickstand.

Without a license, Penelope won't be able to process me as a new hire…*again*. That's gotta be three strikes against me. Looks like instead of playing with paperclips and Post-its tomorrow I'll be filing for unemployment.

Feeling discouraged, I rip the helmet from my head and throw my leg over the side of the bike. I dig into my back pocket for the house key and my stomach growls as I start for the door. Another thing I should've done was stop for food. Neither me nor dad have been here in over month. If there is anything in the fridge, it's probably expired.

"Curly Sue."

No fucking way.

Any moment now the guys with the hidden cameras are going to jump out of the bushes and with any luck I'll be on one of those shows where they offer you a cash prize for scaring the living shit out of you.

I slowly turn around and sure enough, my eyes connect with Marco's. I feel a hint of hysteria creep into my being as I shake my head in disbelief.

"Before you go on and say I'm stalking you, I swear that's not what this is," he defends, and my eyes widen even more.

At this rate, they may just fall out of my head.

"The fact you're standing on my front lawn proves otherwise. What are you doing here—better yet, how the hell do you know where I live?"

"Well—"

"No," I interrupt, raising my hands to my head. I thread my fingers through my curls and take a step closer to him. "Don't answer that. Of course you know where I live, you probably know my blood type and what color underwear I'm wearing too."

He quirks an eyebrow.

"I don't know your blood type but if you want to tell me the color of your underwear, I should probably buy you dinner first."

It takes a lot to render me speechless—well, at least

that's what I thought. Apparently, all it takes is for a cop to stalk me and offer to buy me dinner.

He is offering, right?

I shake my head again, this time a little firmer as I push the ridiculous notion out of my head.

"Look, I have had a day. A really shitty day and there's not much more I can take, so if you're here to give me another ticket or better yet arrest me then do it already," I tell him.

Closing the distance between us, Marco comes to a halt and flashes me a crooked smile. I don't know what is more lethal, that smile or the scent of his cologne. Deciding they're both too much for me right now, I take a step back. What is that thing that everyone talks about? Something about mercury and retrograde, and when it happens, the whole fucking world flips on its axis. Everything spirals out of control. This must be that.

"Mercury is in retrograde and the world is ending," I mumble.

He laughs.

Forget the cologne.

Forget the smile.

His laugh is the most dangerous of all.

I'm so screwed.

"I didn't come here to arrest you, although I suddenly wish I had my handcuffs with me," he teases. He reaches into his back pocket and curiously I narrow my eyes as he brings his hand back around. He lifts my license between his fingers and I feel my blood pressure spike instantly.

The son of a bitch really did steal my license.

CHAPTER FIVE

"Thief!"

The playful smirk falls from my lips as she lunges for me. My instincts kick into gear before she can pluck the license from my fingers and attack me. I wrap my free hand around her wrist and pin it to the small of her back. It's a move I've made countless times, however, I'm usually trying to disarm a man my size, not a svelte little vixen—something I realize the second her body presses against mine.

"Get your hands off of me," she hisses as she glares up at me from the fringe of her long, dark lashes. Enthralled by the fire in her eyes, my fingers tighten around her wrist. I'm about to explain why I have her license and how I went out of my way to get it, but my gaze falls to her lips and I lose all train of thought.

Well, that's not entirely true.

My brain still manages to function to a degree, and I wonder if her lips are as soft as they look. I damn Soraya to hell, because if it wasn't for her filling my head with all that shit earlier, I'd be home watching the Yankee game. Instead, I'm standing here, letting this chick play Russian roulette with my balls.

For real.

Her knee misses the Pirelli family gems by a hair and snaps me out of my fucking trance. Still holding her hands behind her back, I drop my hand that holds her license to my junk and shield my innocent cock from the nutcase itching to put him out of commission.

"Jesus Christ," I growl. "Would you calm the fuck down?"

I come in peace!

"You want me to calm down? First, you pull me over—"

"Oh, for the love of God, not this again," I hiss, shaking my head. At this rate, I'm going to need to make a pit-stop at the church and cleanse my soul from all the swearing and damning the Lord I've been doing since I met this chick.

"Not this again?" she admonishes, her tone rising to heights no one with a New York accent should ever attempt unless they're auditioning for the reboot of Fran Drescher's classic, *The Nanny,* and even then, they should refrain.

"Yes, not this again," I repeat, gritting my teeth. "We both know how the story ends."

I should let her go.

Throw her license at her and get the fuck out of here, but I'm an idiot. An idiot who loosens his hold for a split second because he really digs the fire in her eyes. She takes a step closer and my brain shorts as soon as her thigh brushes against my dick. Not only am I sparring on the front lawn with this crazed girl, but I'm also getting a semi while doing so. If that ain't a sure sign to throw in the towel and run, I don't know what is.

"Yeah, it ends with you manhandling me on my front

lawn after stealing my license and me dropkicking your ass," she spats, blowing a wayward curl from her face.

If I thought she was bluffing, I might let this shit play out, but I'm not about to have my ass. Deciding it's time to set her straight, I release her.

"I didn't fucking steal your license," I grind out. My patience teeters and I think I'm more aggravated with myself than with Antonia. I want to blame Soraya for filling my head, but she didn't suggest I go looking for the license and she sure as fuck isn't the reason I'm here now. Instead of waiting for her to come home, I could've dropped the thing in her mailbox or given it to Soraya.

But, no.

I had to deliver it to her myself.

It's fucking crazy and the longer I stand here trying to convince her I'm not some crazy fucking stalker, the angrier I become.

Frustrated, I comb my fingers roughly through my hair.

"Look, after I left Soraya, I went back to where I pulled you over and found the license in the street." I grab her and turn her palm over, slapping the I.D. card inside. I close her fist around it and drop her hand. "There's gum on the back. Good luck getting it off," I snarl.

Before she can say another word or make any sudden moves that might excite my treacherous dick, I go to leave. I'm two steps away from a clean break when she grabs my arm.

"Wait," she calls.

Again, there's no rhyme or reason for why I pause. Maybe it's stupidity or, better yet, insanity, but I glance at her hand, taking in her slender fingers and the silver rings that decorate them. Tearing my eyes away, I lift my chin and meet her gaze. Surprisingly, she doesn't glare at me. There's a softness there reflected in her eyes and it makes me wonder if there's more to Antonia than leather, a snarky attitude, and road rage.

"You went searching for my I.D.?" she questions.

Oh, good, we're both dumbfucked by my actions.

Sighing, I pull my arm free and shove my hands into my pockets, ignoring the frown that ticks her lips as we both take a step back, putting some distance between us.

"It's not a big deal, okay?" I hiss, feeling slightly ridiculous. As I stand there, feeling her eyes penetrate me, I try to decide how I'm going to explain my actions because I'm sure that's going to be her next question. If the roles were reversed and she hit me with three tickets, I'd want to know why the sudden change of heart too. But I don't think she's gonna buy the insanity plea and unfortunately, *you have a fantastic ass* is not an option.

I like my balls where they are, thank you very much.

I go with a simple response.

"You work for Soraya and I didn't want there to be any bad blood between us. That's it."

Nothing more.

Nothing less.

Bullshit.

She lifts her head and arches one perfect brow, clearly not buying it.

"Next time I won't be so nice," I add.

You know, to really drive the bullshit home.

"Right," she says, lifting the license between us. "Well, thanks."

I jerk my head once and silently will myself to turn around and walk away, but before I can do that, I get distracted. Not by the thundering sound of a motorcycle zooming down the block but by the pensive look on Antonia's face.

"Great," she mutters under her breath "What else can possibly go wrong?"

That seems like a loaded question, one I'm not fucking touching. I follow her gaze, but she quickly slams a hand against my chest, halting me in place. She shoves her license into her back pocket and brings her eyes back to mine.

"I need you to play along."

I'm sorry, come again?

"What?"

"Please," she pleads, hooking me with those big brown eyes. "Besides, you owe me."

Sure I heard her wrong, I bark out a laugh. The engine dies behind me and she slaps my pec a little harder this time.

Alright, so I didn't hear wrong.

"Seriously," she hisses. "You. Owe. Me."

Closing the little distance between us, she lifts her hand from my chest and winds it around the back of my neck. The alarm bells sound somewhere in the back of my head, but I tune them out as soon as my gaze falls to her lips.

"Come on, Officer, pretend I'm your dream girl and look at me like you can't wait to rip my clothes off."

It's not that much of a stretch. I definitely wouldn't mind ripping her clothes off, at least then I might get her to shut up. I also wasn't wrong when I assumed there is more to Antonia than meets the eye and now I know, I know she's fucking nuts. I always did like them a little colorful.

"What the fuck is this?" a deep voice growls from behind me and just like that, I'm pretending to be someone else's boyfriend—at least I think I am. There's got to be a limit as to how many times one man fits the same role in a single lifetime. At this rate, I should put an ad for hire in the newspaper.

Antonia's eyes continue to plead with mine as I mutter

another curse and confession with Father Murphy works its way to the top of my list of things to do.

Sighing, I roll my neck and brace myself to face my audience. Antonia's fingers curl into my neck and she drops her head to my chest and my hands subconsciously grip her hips. Behind every lead actor is a convincing lead actress, and Antonia delivers.

"Get your filthy paws off of her," the guy sneers.

Now, I like to think of myself as a levelheaded man, someone who doesn't let too many people get under his skin. But this guy…*this fucking guy.*

First off, I'm barely touching her. Second, who the hell does this asshole think he is talking to me like that? I lift my hand to the back of my neck and begin to pry Antonia's fingers away so I can deal with the jerkoff behind me, but her hold tightens.

"Hound," she clips, acknowledging the douchebag behind me. She lifts her head from my chest and stares over my shoulder. "I thought I made it clear I didn't want to be followed by anyone."

My brows knit together as I process her words. Suddenly, it all begins to click for me, and I conclude the reason she assumed I was following her is that she's already being stalked by the arrogant tool behind me. Fearing she might be in some kind of trouble, I lower my mouth to her ear and just as I'm about to assure her she's got nothing to worry about, she buries her nose against my cheek.

Damn, she's good.

"Marco and I were just about to go inside," she continues, seductively. "Get lost unless of course, you want to watch."

I don't know who is taunted more by her words, me or the guy she's clearly trying to get a rise out of.

"Antonia," I growl.

Ignoring me, she takes my hand and starts pulling me toward the front door. I dig my heels in place and she shoots me a glare.

"What are you doing?" she hisses.

If we're going to play pretend, we're going to do it right. I would never allow some guy to talk to my girl like he just did, and I sure as fuck wouldn't let her drag me away before I got my own jab in.

"Fuck him, you're coming with me. Get on the back of the bike," dickwad orders.

I was really hoping to walk away from this with my jaw intact, but that's all the son of a bitch has to say for me to lose the little patience I have left. Tearing my hand out of Antonia's, I spin around to face him. I don't get very far though, because his fucking fist collides with my jaw.

Come on!

How is this happening again?

An unintelligible sound erupts from the back of my throat and before he can get another shot, I grab his wrist and pin his arm behind his back, much like I did earlier with Antonia.

"Do you have any idea who you just hit? I'm a—"

My words die as Antonia stomps on my foot. I lose my grip on the animal in front of me and turn to glare at her, but she slams her elbow right into my gut, knocking the wind out of me. I'm getting the shit kicked out of me by my fake girlfriend and her jealous 'hound'. That's what you get for taking an oath to uphold the law and protect the citizens of New York—a fucking day from Hell.

"Jesus fuck," I howl.

I don't know what hurts more, my face, my ribs or my fucking ego. A thought creeps into my mind and with my hands pressed to my knees, I lift my head and look between the two of them, wondering if I'm being played by both sides.

Before I can find out, Antonia brushes past me. My gaze follows her, and I get my first look at Hound as Antonia shoves him back. She starts shouting, but I only make out every other word as I take in the man that towers over her by a good foot or so. His size ain't the only intimidating thing, the motherfucker is covered head to toe in ink, but it's the leather vest and the center patch adorned to it that has me straightening to my full height.

It's the infamous insignia of the Corrupt Hellraisers, and aside from the Satan's Knights, they're the most prominent outlaw motorcycle club this side of the Hudson. Without giving myself a chance to question my actions, I start for the two of them, eager to pull Antonia away from him, but I pause when he tears his eyes from her to look at me.

We stare for a moment, sizing each other up before Antonia turns and starts for me. I don't break eye contact to look at her, though. However, Hound's gaze shoots to Antonia's ass.

It's a sign of weakness and I think he realizes it because he clenches his jaw.

"Come," Antonia calls, taking my hand as she reaches me. Still, I don't move.

Hound spares me another glance before relenting and turning back to his bike. I watch as he throws his leg over his Harley. The motorcycle comes to life as he lifts his kickstand with his boot. He doesn't bother with a helmet and in a flash he skids away from the curb.

Once he's out of sight, I turn my head and stare at Antonia.

"I'm sorry about that," she says as her gaze wanders to

my cheek. Cringing, she lifts her hand to touch the side of my face. "It's already starting to bruise."

"Fuck my cheek," I hiss, wrapping my hand around her wrist. "What the hell was that? How do you know that guy?"

She blows out an exasperated breath, and I drop her hand, watching as she shrugs her shoulders.

"I know him a long time," she replies, cocking her head to the side as she crosses her arms under her chest. "I can handle him if that's what you're wondering."

I don't know what the hell I'm wondering, but I know I don't like that answer.

"Is he your boyfriend?"

She barks out a laugh.

"Definitely not," she responds, still laughing as she uncrosses her arms and reaches into her pocket for her keys. "Look," she continues as she starts for the front door. "Hound thinks he has some type of claim on me, that I'm his responsibility. The sooner he thinks I'm someone else's problem, the sooner he'll back off."

She says it so nonchalantly.

Like it's totally normal for a guy like that to just show up and stake his claim.

She glances over her shoulder at me and pauses. Our eyes lock and she swallows before continuing, "Thanks for being that someone for a minute. I'm really sorry he punched you, oh, and I'm sorry for elbowing you in the stomach and stomping on your foot too."

I think I might have a concussion because I can't formulate a single sentence, all I can do is stare at her. A part of me wants to yell at her, another part wants to shake her, but the biggest part just wants to know her and that's fucking scary for a guy like me.

"I'd offer you ice, but I haven't been home in weeks and

I don't remember the last time I filled the ice trays," she continues, leaning against the door.

She flashes me a smile and it's the first time there isn't a trace of malice, or suspicion and again, I'm fucking winded.

She's got a gorgeous smile.

"Oh, and thanks for bringing me my license. I was a bitch earlier, but, well, you know what kind of day I had. It was really nice of you to go out of your way for me."

"Like I said, it's no big deal."

"Right, because you're friends with my boss."

"Exactly."

She nods.

"Well, maybe you don't tell my boss I elbowed you in the gut and asked you to pretend to be my lover? I've already left a shitty first impression," she says, lowering her thick black lashes.

Instinctively, I reach out and press a finger under her chin, forcing her eyes back to mine.

"I don't know about that," I tell her, admiring her features and committing them to memory.

I was right.

There's definitely more to Antonia DeLuca than meets the eye.

"I think you leave a lot to be desired, Curly Sue," I continue, dropping my hand back to my side. "Maybe I'll see you around."

"Oh, you'll see me for sure," she says, turning to enter the house. Closing the door, she peeks back at me, a smirk toying on her pretty mouth. Her mischievous eyes meet mine and she says, "You'll see me in traffic court when I fight those tickets."

Game on, Curly Sue.

Game fucking on.

CHAPTER SIX

After I got rid of Hound and bid farewell to the hunky cop, I locked myself inside my childhood home and ordered a pizza—half pepperoni, half sausage, the cure to all. By the time I had scarfed down most of the pie and binged an episode of *Criminal Minds*, I was feeling much better. I might even go so far as to say I was relaxed. A rarity for me ever since my dad ordered me to spend my nights at the clubhouse. Coming home, though, giving myself a break from the Corrupt Hellraisers, was just what I needed to recharge.

However, I knew it was only fleeting. Hound didn't show up here last night of his own free will. He's not the type to chase girls. Not when he's looking to get in their pants and sure as hell not after he's done with them. Which is why as soon as I heard the blare of his pipes, I knew my dad had sent him. I also knew he probably ordered Hound to drag me back to the clubhouse, and for a minute there, I expected the beast to do just that—to drag me, kicking and screaming across the lawn until he had me secured to the back of his bike.

That's where Marco came in. I figured if Hound thought I was on a date, he'd relent. Like he doesn't chase girls, he also doesn't fight for them. Well, at least that's what I thought. I didn't expect him to punch Marco in the jaw, but before I could analyze that, Marco fired back and almost revealed he was a cop.

Now, it's one thing for Tank DeLuca's daughter to be with a man outside the club, it's a whole different ballgame for that man to be a police officer. In an attempt to keep him from spilling the beans, I elbowed Marco in the ribs and left him reeling to go deal with Hound. As suspected, he demanded I leave with him. The caveman thing was hot when he was giving me orgasms, but it lost its appeal as soon as he zipped his pants and moved onto the next chick. Hound didn't get to order me around. He didn't get to act as though I was his possession—even if it was all fake and at my father's command, and he certainly didn't get a say in who I dated or fake dated for that matter. Bottom line, Hound needed to back off. We exchanged words, and I offered him front row seats to my pretend night with Marco, which he declined.

Thank fuck for that.

I don't know how I would've pulled that one off. It's one thing to force a cop you barely know to be your boyfriend, it's fucking awkward to follow that act up with asking him to get naked.

Eventually, Hound gave up. He straddled his bike and dragged his pipes to deliver a message to my dad. All I wanted was twenty-four hours of peace. No ex-booty call meddling in my life and no overprotective father trying to control me.

I barely got twelve hours, but it's something.

Sighing, I enter the kitchen and my eyes connect with my dad's. Next time I decide to spend the night as an introvert, I might want to change the locks.

"What are you doing here?" I question, diverting my eyes to the two cups of coffee from Dunkin Donuts he holds in his hands.

"I gave you your time, Tonia," he says, pushing one of the containers toward me.

Lifting my chin, I meet his gaze and note there is an unfamiliar sense of desperation reflected in his eyes. The more I stare, the older he looks, and I start to count the lines on his face, wondering how many of them I've caused and if it compares to how many are a result of his beloved club.

Shaking the thought from my head, I take the coffee and sigh.

"Dad, I can't do this right now. I have to get to work."

"Antonia this can't wait anymore," he says.

From the sound of his tone, I can tell he's losing his patience with me. I just wish I cared.

"Now, I get I might not have been the best father to you, but I tried my hardest. You want to pull away from the club, we can talk about it…*down the road*. Now is not the time to act like a petulant child."

"A petulant child?"

"What, you didn't think your old man knew any fancy words?"

Honestly? No.

But I don't tell him that, not when the vein in his forehead looks like it might explode. He places his cup on the counter and advances toward me.

"Tonia, I'm all for you spreading your wings, but maybe you can do it when the club isn't on the cusp of another street war and we don't have the NYPD's gang unit sniffing around, looking to throw us behind bars," he growls, roughly running his fingers through his salt and pepper hair.

The club is always on the verge of war. If it's not a rival club itching to move in on my dad's territory, it's the mob pushing in or worse, a common street thug looking to make a name for himself. As far as the cop thing goes, of course they're sniffing around. They're always looking to arrest them for one thing or another. If the world ever runs out of toilet paper, they can wipe their asses with all the rap sheets of the Corrupt Hellraisers. That should tide them over.

Meeting his gaze, I lower the coffee cup and swipe my keys from the table.

"With all due respect, Dad, you and I both know they'll never be a time when someone isn't out to get you and asking me to wait to start my life isn't fair." I pause, tearing my eyes away from his because I can't stand the look of regret radiating from them.

I don't mean to make him feel like he's done an inadequate job at raising me. I don't know how to get through to him. If I ask nicely, he pacifies me. More time passes and I remain a fixture in his world.

"For the first time in my life, I'm making my own choices. I'm learning new things and I'm trying to find out what makes me happy. This internship may amount to nothing, but I'm proud of myself for even getting it and I don't want to mess it up, so I'm going to leave now. I'm going to go to work and for eight hours, I'm going to be Antonia DeLuca. Not Tank's daughter, not the princess of the Corrupt Hellraisers—just me."

Whoever that might be.

His jaw ticks and he balls his hands into fists.

"It's not safe," he scolds. "You need to be at the

compound where I can protect you. Not sleeping here and working in some office that I don't have access to." He pauses, and his lip curls in disgust as he grinds out the next sentence. "Hound says you were on a date last night."

There is one thing my dad and I do not discuss and that's my love life. For a criminal who isn't afraid of much, the idea of his little girl getting busy with a man scares the shit out of him. I'm not complaining about it, though.

I was eleven when I got my period for the first time and my father completely lost his shit trying to explain what was happening to me. It was awkward as all hell and the trip to the drugstore that followed scarred me for life. When it came time for me to have my first boyfriend, Dad made Sandy, his girlfriend at the time, take me to the drugstore for condoms. He then had Butch, the road captain of the club, show me how to roll one onto a banana. Yeah, scarred might be putting it lightly. At this stage of the game, I'm not looking to put myself into therapy. The last thing we need is to have a conversation about who I'm sleeping with...or pretending to sleep with.

"So?"

"So..." he fumes. His eyebrows shoot up and his grip tightens around the Styrofoam cup, nearly crushing it. "Where'd you meet him?"

Huffing out a breath, I throw my hands up in frustration.

"What does it matter where I met him?"

"Answer the damn question!" he roars, taking another step forward. He crushes the cup in his hand and doesn't even flinch as the hot liquid spills all over him. The act startles me and I realize this isn't just another power play, this is a dad truly losing his mind over the welfare of his daughter.

I contemplate easing his worry by telling him the truth about Marco and how I used him, but then I'd have to also give up the fact he's a cop and that might make that vein in his forehead burst altogether.

Swallowing, I draw in a deep breath.

"I know you're worried about me, but I'm not going to forfeit a job I might love, to sit here and fight with you. I'll make sure I go to the clubhouse after work and we can talk then."

"You're missing the point, Tonia," he growls. "You going off to work and being out of my sight is dangerous."

"No more than standing idle in a clubhouse waiting for someone to attack," I fire back. "I bet Cash thought his wife was safe there too and that he could protect her, but that's not how their story played out."

It's a low blow and as I watch his shoulders slump with defeat, I instantly regret delivering it. Like we don't talk about my love life, we don't speak of all the carnage his club has caused.

"I'm going to be late," I murmur, grabbing my bag from the back of one of the kitchen chairs. Without giving him another glance, I turn and head for the door.

"Antonia, don't you dare walk away from me."

It's not a demand but rather a plea and it causes me to look back at him.

"We can talk over dinner, okay? Come to some sort of agreement?" I ask hopefully. His eyes bore into mine but he doesn't respond. He simply gives me a jerk of his head and crosses his arms against his chest.

"You're hardheaded," he says, and I smile at him.

As rough as he is, he's got a soft spot for me.

"I wonder where I get that from," I reply.

Sighing, he runs a hand over his face. His eyes meet mine and he gives me a slight shake of his head before muttering something under his breath.

"C'mere," he commands softly.

I don't argue because I know what's coming and when I spin around, I close the distance between us, throwing my arms around my dad's neck as he envelopes me in a great big bear hug.

"Call me as soon as you get in that office, Antonia. I'm not kidding."

As soon as I got into the office, I didn't call my dad. I gave Penelope my license and we got to work with the new-hire papers. An hour later I was officially an employee at the "Ask Ida" advice column with access to the server and the thousands of emails, all from people who were seeking wisdom from Ida.

Soraya was locked in her office on a phone conference with Ida, but she had left specific instructions for me to review past published works. The idea was for me to get a feel for how to respond to the questions in an appropriate manner. Apparently, telling a cheating asshole he should get gangrene on his dick is not an acceptable response for the column.

A little before lunch the door to Soraya's office opens. I tear my eyes away from the cheating scumbag's email and straighten in my chair. Soraya steps out of the office and I immediately note she looks pissed.

"God, that fucking woman is infuriating," she hisses as she flips her long locks over her shoulder. "Penelope!" she bellows. "If Ida calls again, tell her I'm not here."

"Where should I say you went?" Penelope questions.

"I don't care what you tell her. Tell her I died if you

have to, just do not put me on the phone with that woman," Soraya replies.

Whoa.

That's quite the contrast in attitude. Yesterday she was so inviting and understanding, today she's acting as though Ida pissed in her Cheerios.

She must sense me staring because she quickly turns to me. The look of annoyance vanishes from her face as she sighs.

"Oh, good, you're working," she says, heading for my cubicle. "I wasn't sure if you'd be able to get into the system without a license."

My mind instantly wanders back to Marco and I'm even more grateful I didn't have Mouse fix me up with a phony I.D.—that would be fun to explain to my already pissed boss. Forcing a smile, I shrug my shoulders.

"So, a funny thing happened last night...when I got home Officer Pirelli was waiting for me with my license."

Her dark eyebrows arch curiously and she leans a hip against my cubicle.

"Marco had your license?"

"Yeah, he said he went back to where he pulled me over and found it lying in the middle of the street. Crisis averted."

A devilish grin works her lips as she crosses her arms under her chest.

"Is that right?" she questions, smugly.

I think I like angry Soraya better. The cat who ate the canary look doesn't really suit her and I don't feel comfortable having her assume there is something going on between me and her friend. Sure, it was nice of him to give me my license, and I'll even give him some points for playing the role of my boyfriend, but that's it. We've got a date in traffic court, and I plan on beating those tickets—I don't care how hot he is.

Attempting to divert the conversation, I turn my computer screen toward her, but she doesn't take the bait.

"What?" I question.

She shakes her head.

"Nothing," she replies.

"Right, okay, so…these submissions are—"

My words get cut off as Penelope's voice sounds.

"Soraya, Marco—er, I mean, Mr. Pirelli, is on holding for you on line two."

The shit-eating grin spreads wider on Soraya's face and I silently curse Marco as she turns on her heel and heads back into her office to take the call. When she's out of sight, I slam my head against the keyboard.

"Speak of the devil, and he will appear."

CHAPTER SEVEN

You know you're fucked when you spend the better part of the night with a bag of frozen peas pressed to your cheek. Bringing Antonia her license was a mistake, but I couldn't stay away. I wanted more of that wild woman and as I nursed a six-pack of beer and tended to my bruised jaw, I decided one chance encounter wasn't enough.

I wanted Antonia DeLuca in my bed.

I wanted her writhing beneath me, screaming my name and begging me for more.

Convincing myself I was drunk, I pushed those thoughts out of my head and forced myself to go to sleep. I figured I'd wake up a new man. I'd forget all about the hot-blooded vixen that sent a typical Monday into a fucking tailspin.

But you know what they say, drunk words are sober thoughts. When my alarm sounded, I opened my eyes to find my hand wrapped around my cock and like a fool, I turned, expecting to see Antonia beside me.

Dreams, man, they'll fuck you up.

I dragged myself out of bed, took a shower and the whole fucking time I struggled to keep her out of my mind and my hands off my junk. By the time I got to the precinct, thoughts of her resurfaced. This time she wasn't naked and sweaty from having been fucked six ways to Sunday, she was with that sleazy biker, Hound, and my mind kept replaying the same words over and over.

"Hound thinks he has some type of claim on me, that I'm his responsibility."

That's a pretty big stand for a man to take when he's not her boyfriend. I didn't like it and instead of typing up my reports, I found myself digging into the database for information on this Hound character. I didn't have a real name for the asshole, so I did a search on the Corrupt Hellraisers, but before the system could pull any hits, I got called out on a domestic dispute.

Prying into Antonia's life would have to wait.

My partner, Richie, and I hit the patrol car and sped to the location dispatched over the radio. There we found a disgruntled wife setting her husband's clothes on fire because he forgot to pay the cable bill. Reason seven-hundred and thirty-six not to get married.

Women are fucking nuts, they flip on a dime and still, as Richie got on the radio with the fire department, I couldn't help but think of Antonia. She's definitely the type to set a man's boxers on fire along with the begonias.

Once the fire department came and put the fire out, we took the husband's statement.

"Ten bucks says he's back in the house tomorrow," Richie says as we finally pull away from the house.

"Twenty says we're here next week," I counter.

He shakes his head as he turns the corner.

"If Tina ever lit my shit on fire, I'd run for the hills."

Raising an eyebrow, I turn to him. He's full of shit. If Richie's wife set his clothes on fire, he'd fuck her into next week. Like me, the guy gets off on crazy. It's the reason he's on his fourth wife. The first three were too timid. Tina keeps things interesting and Marco prefers a woman who raises hell from time to time.

We're alike in that regard.

I like a woman who isn't afraid to express herself. Someone who will challenge me and keep me on my toes. I'd prefer she not light my shit on fire, but if I deserved it, if I played her dirty—well, I'd expect nothing less.

Again, my mind drifts to Antonia. The fact that I can't shake her alarms me, but I ignore it as I begin to wonder if that dickhead, Hound, did her dirty.

Muttering a curse, I divert my gaze away from Richie and swipe a hand over my face. The second my palm grazes the bruise on my jaw, I flinch, and Richie notices.

"You gonna tell me what happened, or should I take a guess?" he questions.

I really don't want to get into it with him. The guy is relentless. If I tell him I went out of my way to bring a girl her license and got my ass handed to me, it will be all over the department. I'll be hazed for weeks and I'm not looking to relive my days of being a rookie. No fucking thank you. I did my time.

"It's nothing."

"Bullshit. Who'd you piss off this time?"

"This time? You make it sound like this is a regular occurrence," I grunt.

If I was having this conversation with my cousin, Tig, he'd say this is a regular occurrence and remind me I was Graham's punching bag too.

That's what you get for helping a friend.

No one lets you live it down.

Richie doesn't know I took a hit from Soraya's husband, though. I start to think that makes him the perfect candidate to confide in. Lord knows I need someone to straighten me out and the hazing might be worth it if it means putting Antonia out of my head once and for all.

"I met this girl…pulled her over yesterday and gave her three tickets."

His eyebrows shoot up and I can tell he's struggling not to laugh in my face.

"A chick gave you that shiner?"

"No, you jackass," I hiss, gritting my teeth. "Her boyfriend did." I pause and shake my head. "Hell, he's not even her boyfriend. I don't know what the fuck he is."

"So, wait, let me see if I got this straight. You pull some girl over, give her three tickets and her man takes a fist to your face?"

"Not exactly," I groan, preparing myself for the cackling that's about to ensue as soon as I tell him the whole sordid tale. "I told you about the anniversary party for Tig and Delia that Soraya roped me into helping her plan, remember?"

"Yeah," he replies, narrowing his eyes. He slows for the red light and turns to me, giving me his undivided attention. "Well, yesterday I had to meet her for lunch to discuss the party and when I got to the office to pick her up, I discovered the girl I pulled over was Soraya's new intern."

"So?"

"So, apparently she dropped her license when I pulled her over and accused me of stealing it."

A grin teases the corner of his lips as he flips his gaze back to the street.

"Oh, this is too good."

"Shut up, dick."

Fighting the smirk, he clears his throat.

"I'm sorry, go ahead."

I'd take a fucking bullet for him, but that doesn't mean I have to like him. In fact, right now, I can't fucking stand him.

"Anyway, after I convinced her I didn't take her license, I went to lunch with Soraya as planned but I couldn't stop thinking about her and even if I could, Soraya wasn't gonna let me."

I pause, recalling our conversation and the text she sent once she left.

Send her an edible fruit arrangement

It's not a terrible idea.

Before I realize what I'm doing, I reach for my cell phone and pull up Soraya's number.

"What are you doing?" Richie questions.

I have no fucking idea, but when a woman consumes your every waking thought, you need to do something. The only way to get her out of my head is to get my fill of her. Then I won't spend every minute wondering how she tastes. I'll quit thinking about wrapping all that wild hair of hers around my fist and I'll stop imaging what sounds she makes when she comes.

Jesus.

It's worse than I thought.

"Dude, you're sweating," Richie comments. "Are you having a heart attack or something? A stroke, maybe?"

Ignoring him, I press the phone to my ear.

One night, that should do it. The dreams will come to an end, my dick will calm the fuck down and I won't do ridiculous shit like searching the rap sheets of criminals she may or may not have fucked.

I listen as the phone rings and my gaze snaps back to Richie.

"What do you know about the Corrupt Hellraiser's MC?"

He blinks.

"Don't look at me like that," I warn. I pull the phone away from my ear when no one answers, making sure I dialed the right number. "Why the fuck is no one answering?"

"I take one day off," Richie mutters and I turn back to him. "One day and you lose your mind."

Tell me about it.

The receptionist answers the phone and I quickly ask for her to connect me to Soraya's private line.

"Are your ears ringing?" Soraya greets.

"Come again?"

"Well, Antonia and I were just talking about you," she reveals. "I hear you were quite the good cop yesterday. Not too many officers would go out of their way to bring a woman their license after hitting her with three tickets."

"Yeah, I'm a catch," I mumble. "Should I relay that message?" she quips.

"Funny. If the advice column thing takes a dive, you should give stand up comedy a whirl," I retort. "You got any more jabs you want to take, or can we get to why I'm calling?"

"You better be calling me to tell me you figured out a way to get Tig and Delia to the party."

I roll my eyes.

This is the first, and last time I voluntarily subject myself to planning a party. Actually, I take that back. I love a good party. Take the Super Bowl, for instance. I go all out for the big game. There's a four-foot hero, wings for days and beer on tap. I even decorate my apartment with vintage football jerseys and buy football shaped paper plates. I'm telling you, I throw a mean party.

It's surprise anniversary parties that just aren't my thing.

"I'm working on it," I mutter.

Lies.

Straight fucking lies.

"Marco…" she warns.

"I'll get them there," I promise. I'm not above arresting them and dragging them to the restaurant. Whatever it takes, I got this—that's if I get my head screwed on straight. "I need your help."

"With?"

"Antonia."

"I knew it!"

"Please don't gloat. It's not very becoming," I say. Richie laughs silently beside me, and I flip him the bird. "Will you help me or not?" I sigh.

"Depends what you need," she retorts cheekily.

I remain silent. I can't believe I'm doing this.

"Marco," Soraya calls. "I don't have all day."

Muttering a curse, I grip the phone tightly and grind out my request.

"How do I send an edible fruit arrangement?"

Go ahead, laugh.

Richie does.

"You're pathetic," Richie says, as he takes a seat on top of my desk. Slightly startled, I peel my eyes away from my cell phone and look at him. He lifts the cold, half-eaten slice of pizza from my paper plate and takes a huge bite.

"I was eating that," I point out.

Chewing, he shrugs his shoulders and folds the slice. He drains the oil from it before taking another bite. With his mouth full, he answers.

"No, you weren't. You're too busy staring at your phone to bother with food."

This is true.

After Soraya had a good laugh at my expense, a call came over the radio. Richie and I had to respond to a robbery in progress, so I hung up with her and switched into cop mode. I don't think I've ever been so happy to chase a perp down Canal Street and it was a welcome distraction from the fact I had just coerced my friend into sending her intern a bouquet of fresh fruit.

When we returned to the precinct with the perp, I called Soraya, but she was on a conference call and couldn't get on the phone with me. On top of that, the woman isn't answering my texts, so I have no idea if she sent the arrangement. I wonder if the receptionist will hang up on me if I call the office again.

I lean back against my chair and fold my hands behind my head as Richie pops the last bite of crust into his mouth.

"Soraya isn't answering me," I explain.

"Do me a favor, if I ever tell you I'm bored with Tina, remind me of today," he says, wiping his mouth with the back of his hand. "I don't miss this nonsense." With an exasperated sigh, he points a finger at the phone in my hand. "Stop being a pussy and ask for the girl you want to talk to and leave Soraya out of it. Cut through the bullshit and be a fucking man for Christ's sake."

"To be fair, I'm not usually like this," I defend.

"No, you're not. Which tells me you're either in over your head or you've met your match."

I find the latter part of that sentence is disturbing.

"Bite your tongue," I hiss, considering his first theory.

Antonia is a smoke show, but I'm overly invested and that might be why I don't like the idea of her hanging around a guy like Hound. Just like the man in me can't stop thinking about her sweet ass and perfect tits, the cop in me can't ignore the fact she might be in trouble. I know she thinks she's capable of handling a guy like that, but let's face it, he's a criminal. God only knows what he's capable of.

I look back at Richie.

"You never answered me before when I asked you about the Corrupt Hellraisers," I point out.

He raises an eyebrow.

"You were serious about that?"

"Contrary to popular belief, I don't speak just to hear myself talk." I drop my hands from behind my head and straighten in my chair. "When I dropped off her license a guy from the club showed up at Antonia's house. She was pretty pissed at him and made it like we were on a date. That's who gave me the shiner."

Richie quirks an eyebrow and crosses his arms against his chest.

"So, you think this girl is mixed up with the club, that's why you're running in circles, ordering chocolate dipped fruit on a stick."

I think about that for a second. Before I searched the database this morning, I tried to rationalize what I was about to do. I told myself I wasn't looking to single-hand-edly take down a bunch of bikers. Hell, I'm not even looking to take down one. I'm just a nosy prick who doesn't like the idea of another man sniffing around something I have an interest in.

Right?

Shaking my head, I picture her face. Those eyes. That mouth. All that wild hair.

The things I'd do to her.

One night.

That's all I need.

"She's hot as fuck too," I add. "And she's feisty. Light your shit on fire kind of feisty. But you don't care because you know she's one of a kind and you're the lucky bastard who gets her, so you ignore the crazy."

He nods.

I knew he'd get it.

"I'm putting in for a new partner," he deadpans. "You've lost your fucking mind."

Possibly. A sane man would walk away and forget he ever laid eyes on Antonia DeLuca. He'd tell himself the girl is the definition of trouble and if a man isn't careful, he'll lose himself to her before he even gets a taste.

Yeah, Richie's right.

I've lost it.

But it'll be a cold day in Hell before I admit that.

"I got the perp, didn't I?" I say instead.

"What perp?"

Surprised, Richie and I both turn at the sound of Tony Dinaso's voice. We met in the academy and instantly hit it off. There aren't too many boys in blue who share a fondness for hair gel and after we graduated, we managed to remain tight despite being appointed to different precincts.

A couple of months ago, Tony got transferred to our precinct and promoted to the Gang Intelligence Unit. Sergeant Floyd felt Tony was a good fit for a sting operation he was working on and for the last two months Tony has been shadowing one of the soldiers of the Bendetti crime family.

"Oh, look what the cat dragged in," Richie quips.

"You pinch Bendetti?" I ask.

"Not exactly," he replies, lifting his eyes from the file he's flipping through. He meets my gaze and points a finger at my cheek. "What happened to you?"

Richie chuckles and I shoot him a glare. Before I can warn him to keep his big trap shut, the desk sergeant shouts for me.

"Hey, Pirelli! You got a visitor."

CHAPTER EIGHT

MARCO

"WHAT THE HELL IS THIS, huh?" Antonia questions as I reach the front desk.

I barely have a chance to process the fact that she's standing in my precinct before her eyes lock with mine and I lose all train of thought. Those fucking eyes, man, even when there is a murderous gleam radiating from them—they're hypnotizing.

Clearing my throat, I pull myself together as she huffs out a breath and shoves the oversized bouquet of fruit toward me. Jesus, leave it to Soraya. Talk about overkill. This thing probably costs a fortune, and Antonia doesn't even look all that impressed.

Lifting my chin, I stare at her over the top of the bouquet.

"Looks like some cantaloupe, pineapple…oh, and the green stuff is honeydew," I reply, reaching out to pluck a piece of melon from one of the sticks. Popping it in my mouth, I grin at her.

"I know what it is," she hisses, pushing it at me again. "What I want to know is why you sent it to me!"

Fearing she might send the fruit across the precinct, I take the bouquet from her and raise an eyebrow at her.

"You don't like fruit?"

"It's melon," she argues, gritting her teeth.

"Okay," I reply slowly. "So, you don't like melon then."

"I like melons just fine," she snaps and angrily slams her palm against the desk. My brain short circuits following the movement and my gaze gets stuck on the Johnny Cash tee stretched across her chest.

"Yeah, I'm a fan myself," I confess.

Of both Mr. Cash and melons—specifically hers.

"I don't know what you're up to…"

"I'm not up to anything," I tell her. Admitting I'm using produce to get into her pants will only send her running. I pull out a piece of pineapple and offer the stick to her. "Try it."

She narrows her eyes for a split second before dropping her gaze to the piece of fruit. Pulling the pineapple off the stick, she pops it into her mouth. A satisfied grin spreads across my mouth until she closes her eyes and moans loudly. The busy precinct seems to come to a standstill, and everyone turns their attention to Antonia.

"Oh…yes…so…good."

Her eyes open and lock with mine as her pink tongue sneaks out and runs along her lips. My hands tighten around the bouquet as I struggle to remain unaffected by her shenanigans. My dick doesn't get the memo though, and twitches against the zipper of my jeans. The boys in blue hoot and holler as I bite back a groan and a smug expression washes over Antonia's face.

"What's your game, Pirelli?" she asks as she crosses her arms against her chest. I lose the battle, and my gaze lowers.

"Eyes up here, officer," she snaps. "Answer me."

"Uh…what was the question?"

"Why did you send me an edible fruit arrangement?"

Shrugging, I set the bouquet on the desk and glance around the packed precinct. Everyone with a badge is waiting for me to respond, including Richie and Tony. I focus on my partner.

"Can you finish booking the perp?"

He gives me a nod and I turn to the desk sergeant, Judy. She's in her late sixties and a bitter old tool who hates me. Seriously, I've tried my hardest to get the broad on Team Pirelli. I bring her coffee in the morning and last Valentine's day, I got her a box of Godiva chocolates. She told me she threw them in the trash, but I caught her stuffing her face in the break room later that day.

"Hey, Sarg," I call, flashing her a grin. I don't know if she's lost control over her facial expressions or if she's had too much Botox, but she never smiles. Actually, that's not true. She smiled the other day when I fell down the stairs.

"Here, this is for you," I say, pushing the fruit toward her.

"Hold up," Antonia interjects. "You mean to tell me I carried that ridiculous thing on the subway so you could give it to her? Oh, hell no."

Judy takes the arrangement from me just as Antonia lunges for it.

"Give me back my melons," she demands, leaning over the desk.

"You heard the man," Judy says. "They're my melons now."

Biting the inside of my cheek, I suppress a laugh and step around the desk so that I'm standing beside Antonia.

"Enjoy, Judy," I call over my shoulder as I take hold of Antonia's elbow. "Let's go, Curly Sue."

I start to lead her away from the desk, but she pulls free. Turning to me, she pushes both her hands against my chest and gives me a hard shove.

"I'm not going anywhere with you! You just gave that old lady my edible fruit arrangement!"

I flinch at her choice of words and quickly take her hands from my chest, lacing her fingers together.

"You just called Judy an old lady. We better make a run for it."

I'm only partially teasing but considering Judy isn't rushing to kill Antonia, I think she might've missed the dig. To my surprise, though, Antonia doesn't snatch her hands away from mine.

Look at us making progress.

Testing the waters some more, I pull her closer. She lifts her chin and stares up at me skeptically and as predicted, I get lost in those brown eyes.

"Fuck the fruit. Let me take you to dinner, instead."

Her eyes widen and she looks at me as though I just suggested we take a trip to the moon. Then she bursts out laughing.

"What?"

"Dinner," I repeat, firmer this time.

The way I see it, a woman doesn't drag a bundle of fruit across Manhattan for no good reason. The moment she received the delivery she could've pulled a Judy and chucked the arrangement into the nearest trash can. Instead, she's standing in my precinct, staring at me with those come fuck me eyes.

That's gotta count for something.

"There's this little Italian place on the corner, they make a mean meatball hero," I continue, keeping my eyes pinned to hers as I give her hands a squeeze. "Or do you have something against meat too?"

Shaking her head, she tears her gaze away from me and pulls her hands free.

Fuck, please don't let her be a vegetarian. That might kill me.

"I can't," she whispers as she lifts her hand and combs her fingers through her curls.

Damn, what I would give to do that.

Focus, Pirelli.

"I have to go," she adds. "I shouldn't have come here." She tries to brush past me but my instincts kick into gear and I grab her wrist.

Fuck that.

"Tell me why," I demand softly.

Sighing, she looks to the spot where my fingers touch her soft skin before her gaze wanders around the precinct, reminding me we have an audience, and judging by the expression on her face, it's an unwelcome one. Her eyes slice back to mine.

"Because you're a cop."

Narrowing my eyes, I ask, "So?"

A frown ticks the corners of her lips drawing my attention to that perfect mouth.

"So, I don't date cops," she explains.

Well, it was perfect until those words came flying out of it. Of course she doesn't date cops. Only criminals that have ridiculous names like Hound. Biting the inside of my cheek, I look away and cringe realizing my entire precinct just witnessed me getting shut down by a chick.

That kind of humiliation would be enough for any other man to tuck tail, but not me.

"Let's do this outside."

It's not really a suggestion since I don't give her a chance to debate. With a quick tip of my chin in Richie's direction, I signal to him that I'm done for the day and take Antonia's hand, escorting her out of the precinct. Once we hit the sidewalk, I release her hand and turn to face her.

She tucks her hair behind her ears and shakes her head.

"Look, it's nothing personal, Marco." She stops herself. "I mean, yesterday, I would've said otherwise, but then you showed up at my house with my license—"

I cut her off. "Just in time to make your boyfriend jealous."

"I told you, Hound isn't my boyfriend," she snaps. Blowing out an exasperated breath, she cocks her head to the right. "What I'm trying to say is you're not a bad guy. Yeah, you suck at first impressions, but you're easy on the eyes…" her voice trails and she offers me a wink. It's cute as fuck—so is the little smile teasing her lips. "Ok, really easy on the eyes," she amends before continuing. "…and you sent me an edible fruit arrangement, which was really sweet, but you're a cop!"

Sweet.

She thinks I'm sweet.

"Aww, you think I'm sweet," I mock through gritted teeth. Taking a step closer, I touch a finger to her chin and force her eyes back to mine. Shaking my head, I continue, "I didn't send you that fucking thing to be sweet, Antonia. I sent it because I can't get you out of my fucking head. I sent it because I woke up this morning wondering what you taste like. What your body feels like. And fuck me, I couldn't stop myself from imagining what sounds you might make when I make you come undone. When you're writhing beneath me, begging for more."

That perfect mouth of hers forms an O, and a gasp flies out.

"But no worries," I go on, taking a step back. I hold up my hands and shrug my shoulders. "You don't date cops and I don't chase girls who don't want to be chased." Shoving my hands in my pockets, I glance toward the street.

Hell, at this point maybe she's doing me a favor seeing as she's got me this wound up and all I've done is hold her hand. There's no way one night with her would be enough and I'm not looking to make a fool out of myself any more than I already have.

That's what you get for thinking with your dick.

"Marco…" she murmurs.

Done with this conversation, I shake my head. Reaching into my back pocket, I pull out my keys. I'm about to walk away from her when I remember she said she took the subway here. Muttering a curse, I close my fist around the keys and look at her.

"Where's your bike?" I grunt.

"Back at the parking garage. I couldn't carry the arrangement in my saddlebags, so I took the train…" her voice trails as she brushes the hair away from her eyes. "Forget that…" she stammers. "Marco, you can't say stuff like that and then just ask me where my bike is," she argues.

"Sure I can," I reply, grabbing her elbow. I start to lead her down the street, toward the lot where my car is parked.

"Here's how this is going to play out, I'm giving you a ride back to the office and then we can go our separate ways. No more advances. If I stop at the office to see Soraya and you're there, I'll say hello, but you have my word, no more melons."

"But I like melon," she protests.

For crying out loud, this girl is making me dizzy.

One minute she's hot, the next she's cold.

I can't keep up.

"And I really like meatball sandwiches."

I turn to her and she flashes me a smile, the kind of smile you feel deep down in your bones. One you know you'll never recover from. A smile that will change the entire course of your life if you let it.

Shit.

Inching closer, she tilts her head back and looks up at me.

"And I really like all that dirty talk too, Officer Pirelli."

Swallowing, I stare back at her.

"That wasn't dirty talk."

"Oh?"

This girl is going to ruin me.

Obliterate me.

She's going to leave me in a million fucking pieces.

"You want dirty talk, keep smiling at me like that and I'll give you all the filthy words you can imagine."

CHAPTER
NINE

ANTONIA

MONDAY MIGHT BE A BITCH, but her sister, Tuesday, is well on her way to becoming a total twat. At this rate, I'm scared to see what Wednesday is going to bring and let's not even talk about Friday. By then I should either be fired, married, or fucked.

Literally.

Things were going well for the most part until I revealed Marco as my knight in shining armor to Soraya. There was no mistaking the gloating expression on her face and I immediately fell victim to foot in mouth syndrome. I went from being fully immersed in my work to daydreaming about Marco. I wound up pushing some of the most ridiculous emails through to Soraya's and, yeah, you guessed it, I cc'd Ida on them too.

That pink slip was inevitable.

But Tuesday wasn't done. In fact, she left the biggest plot twist for the end of the day. I was powering off my computer, when a deliveryman stepped off the elevator asking for me.

My first thought was that my dad had come to his senses and decided to send me something to congratulate me on my new gig. We may be at odds, but he's still the guy who showed up to every dance recital with the largest bouquet of pink roses, so it wasn't that far of a stretch.

I never imagined Marco would send me something and when the delivery guy asked me to sign, I brought the arrangement straight into Soraya's office. I mean, it was only logical to assume he was sending her, his friend, someone he knew longer than twenty-four hours, a bouquet of fresh fruit and not me, the girl he just met. It's not like we even hit it off or anything. As far as first meetings go, ours was a disaster and totally unworthy of chocolate dipped goodness.

I set the arrangement down on Soraya's desk, and she looked at me with confusion. Since I had sent her one yesterday to apologize for my tardiness, she must've thought it was from me, that it was some sort of calling card and my go-to plan for ass kissing.

"Why are you giving that to me?" she asked.

"It's yours," I said with a shrug. "Marco sent it to you."

"Um, no he didn't."

The girl was in denial and I couldn't blame her. I imagine her husband wouldn't be too keen on her coming home with another fruit arrangement, especially knowing a man sent it to her. Friend or not, it was weird and shame on Marco for making the moves on a married woman.

"Marco sent that to you," she said pointedly. "Read the card."

My cheeks flamed as she plucked the card from the arrangement that had *my* name on it and handed it to me. Ripping it open, I turned my back to her and read the card.

I don't want to wait until traffic court to see you again.

I read it three times and each time it became harder to ignore the unfamiliar warmth creeping into the pit of my stomach. Then embarrassment flooded me, and I grew defensive. Guys didn't do this. Most of the men I dated were morally compromised in one fashion or another, and they surely didn't abide by those old-school values most women look for in a man. Hell, I'm not even sure men like that exist in the real world anymore.

The point I'm trying to make is, men, don't send me gifts and little notes expressing their desire to see me. I'm not sure if that's because men don't perceive me as a girl worthy of such sweet gestures, or if I've just sold myself short by choosing to let the wrong guys into my life.

You're probably thinking I'm overreacting. Hell, at this point you're probably calling me a bitch and internally shouting for me to just accept the gift and shut the fuck up. But when a girl isn't used to being treated a certain way, I think it's only natural for her to assume the worst. And let's not forget, I've been groomed not to trust anyone with a badge since I came out of my mother's womb.

So, convinced Marco had an ulterior motive, I grabbed the bouquet from Soraya's desk and asked her where I could find him. At the time I didn't think anything of it, but looking back now, I should've realized she was all too eager to give up his precinct. She even told me what train I should take to make sure I caught him before he left for the day.

There was only standing room on the train so you can imagine how bizarre I looked juggling the monstrosity of fruit in my arms while still trying to hold on to the stanchion. I was the laughingstock of the caboose. By the time I entered the precinct I was sure I looked like a madwoman without a plan.

I made my way toward the desk where a scary woman stood scowling at me like I was a piece of gum on her shoe. Civic hero, my ass. The second I asked for Marco, she muttered a curse under her breath and shouted for him. Apparently, she wasn't a fan of the gifty cop either.

As soon as he came into my view, I knew I had made a major mistake. Instead of wondering what Marco's motives might be, I should've anticipated how I'd feel the moment our eyes locked. But one thing is certain, I never could've prepared myself for how my whole body would heat under the spell of his dirty promises.

"I can't get you out of my fucking head. I sent it because I woke up this morning wondering what you taste like. What your body feels like. And fuck me, I couldn't stop myself from imagining what sounds you might make when I make you come undone. When you're writhing beneath me, begging for more."

So here I am, in a quaint little Italian restaurant, sitting across from Marco at a tiny table draped with a red and white checkered tablecloth while Frank Sinatra croons on a speaker in the background. I have no idea what I'm doing, but walking away, pretending like our paths never crossed, seems more terrifying than sharing a meal with him.

Feeling the weight of his stare, I carefully avoid eye contact and reach for another breadstick. When in doubt, load up on carbs.

"So," I start, clearing my throat before I take a bite of the breadstick. "…you and Soraya are close, huh?" I ask with my mouth full. Very ladylike, I know. Did I forget to mention I'm awkward when I'm nervous? Not only am I chewing like a cow, but I am also sweating like a pig too.

It's really no wonder I attract animals like Hound.

Giving me an easy smile, he pushes the basket of focaccia and breadsticks closer to me.

"If you think the breadsticks are good, you should try

the focaccia and dip it in the infused olive oil," he suggests, reaching to grab a piece for himself.

I stop chewing and watch as he dunks the bread in the olive oil—not once, but three times. Once it's dripping with Italian liquid gold, he leans over the table and takes a huge bite. A moan erupts from the back of his throat, and my thighs clench together at the sound. You know you have dived into the deep end when you find a man eating a piece of bread as a form of foreplay.

"Damn that's good," he praises, lifting his glass of water from the table. He brings it to his mouth and nearly empties the glass in one gulp. I divert my eyes to his neck, watching as he swallows.

Damn, that's sexy too.

Setting the glass down, he clears his throat and I feel my cheeks flame as I take a piece of the focaccia.

"Where were we...oh, right, Soraya?" he shrugs noncommittally. "I've known her since we were kids. Me, her, and my cousin Tig all grew up in the same neighborhood. Things changed once Tig met his wife, Delia, though. The three of them remained tight, but I kind of just went off on my own. Then a couple of years ago, when she and Graham were first starting out, they hit a rough patch. She and Tig suckered me into pretending to be her boyfriend."

I stop dunking the bread in the oil and lift my eyes to his.

"You're kidding," I accuse.

He shakes his head and laughs, pointing a finger toward the side of his face.

"Graham broke my jaw, and they lived happily ever after."

"Oh God," I groan, slapping a palm to my forehead. "And last night was a cheap reenactment," I add, pulling my hand away.

Our eyes lock.

"A cheap reenactment?" he questions.

"Yeah, at least Soraya was a friend, I'm a stranger. Big difference."

He shrugs his shoulders and taps his knuckles against the table as a gorgeous smile spreads across his lips.

"Well, we're changing that now, aren't we?" he probes.

"I guess we are," I reply, returning the smile.

The waiter, a little old man with bushy eyebrows and thinning gray hair, appears to take our order. The name embroidered to his apron says Luigi. As she and Marco chat I learn he's the owner of the restaurant and the man behind the killer meatball hero.

Both men praise one another before Luigi turns to me and thanks me. Apparently, Marco isn't a fan of dining alone and always takes his food to go. Tonight, is the first time Luigi is having the pleasure of serving his favorite patron. I don't know why I find that so surprising. You would think there's a long list of girls who'd happily go to dinner with him.

"We'll take two meatball parm heroes on garlic bread and go heavy on the fresh mootz." He pauses and turns to me. "Would you like something else to drink?" he questions, tipping his chin toward the glass of water sitting in front of me. "Luigi's wife makes a mean glass of sangria."

"Ah, si, molto bene," Luigi says.

Pulling my lower lip between my teeth, I stare back at Marco. It's tempting.

"I shouldn't drink."

"Why not?" Marco questions. "I can drive you home."

Someone calls for Luigi and he excuses himself, promising to return with a pitcher of Sangria and more focaccia. I look back at Marco and he raises an eyebrow waiting me to respond to his question.

If this was a date between two normal people that would be ideal, but my bike is at the office and even if it wasn't, Marco dropping me off at the compound would be a disaster. Forget Hound, he'd have to field questions from the entire club, including my dad. I think I'll stick with the water.

"Another time, my bike is at the garage," I say.

"Already thinking about another time, huh?"

Realizing my slipup, I roll my eyes and Marco just smirks.

I wonder how many girls have lost their panties to that grin.

"I guess it all depends on whether Luigi's meatball parm hero lives up to my expectations or not," I answer.

"You'll be moaning in twenty minutes," he says confidently.

"You sound sure."

Propping his thick forearms on the table, he leans forward.

"There are two things guaranteed to make you moan. The first is Luigi's meatballs, the second is me. It's going to take him twenty minutes to plate our food, that gives us time to sneak into the bathroom and test the second theory."

My stomach flips at the suggestion and I lick my lips. If this is a test, I'm going to fail epically. You see, the thing about dating morally challenged guys is there are no expectations. You know they're a dime a dozen and if they walk away, you don't really care. No big loss. But the guy who sends you fruit and takes you to a little hole in the wall restaurant where he introduces you to the owner, you're not so quick to write him off. You realize guys like him don't come around all that often and when they do, they're looking for a specific girl. For the first time in my life, I care whether I fit the mold or not and that scares me, because I wasn't expecting any of this.

"I'm disappointed," Marco says. "I was sure you'd either call my bluff or tell me to fuck off."

My gaze snaps back to him.

"I'm thinking."

It's a lame response, but it bides the time.

"The clock is ticking, but we can weigh the options. I don't need the whole twenty minutes to get you moaning." Still leaning close, he cocks his head to the side. "Five minutes should do."

A smile forms on my lips.

"You're cocky."

"And you're stalling."

"Observant too."

"What can I say, I'm a catch."

Yeah, he is.

Biting the inside of my cheek, I stare at him for a beat. Just as I'm about to respond and tell him he's got two minutes, not five, my cell phone rings. I peel my eyes from Marco and twist around to pull my phone from my leather jacket that's draped over the back of the chair. Pulling it out, I turn it over and cringe when I see my father's number.

"Shit," I hiss.

I forgot all about our dinner plans.

Silencing the call, I regretfully turn back to Marco.

"I'm so sorry, but I have to go." Pushing back my chair, I quickly rise and pull my jacket on. "I have this thing…and I completely forgot. I…" I stop rambling when he stands. "What are you doing?"

Ignoring my question, he looks toward the kitchen.

"Luigi! Make the order to go," he shouts to the sweet old man. Reaching into his pocket, he pulls out a few bills and tucks them between the salt and pepper shakers. He lifts his head and continues, "I'll take you back to your bike."

"You don't have to do that."

"Of course I don't," he says evenly. "But I'm going to anyway and you're going to give me your number so we can do this the right way. Without any interruptions."

"You're not going to ask where I have to be?"

"No. It doesn't matter to me because I know no matter where you go and what you do, you'll be wishing you were locked in a bathroom with me for five minutes."

He leaves me standing beside the table and disappears into the kitchen. A minute later he returns with two brown paper bags. Offering me one, he gently touches his free hand to the small of my back before nodding toward the door.

Yeah, Marco Pirelli is definitely not the norm for me.

He's the guy you hope sticks.

Too bad a girl like me can never keep a guy like him.

CHAPTER TEN

ANTONIA

"Okay, Antonia, pull it together and stop smiling," I murmur to myself. I can't walk into the clubhouse with a grin on my face when I'm late to have dinner with my dad, that would just be a slap in the face to him. Besides, I'm not the smiley type. If I walk in there with a shit-eating grin, everyone will ask questions.

If they knew a man was the cause of my smile all hell would break loose.

Some of the guys, the younger ones who are close to my age, would crack endless jokes. The old-timers, the guys who took the oath with my dad, wouldn't find it so funny and they would be out for blood. Hound would be a wild-card, though. He'd likely be swayed to my dad's side and not because he's got some undying attachment to me. The man is so far up my old man's ass, it's hard to tell where he begins and my dad ends. He'd also put two and two together, figure it was Marco and my smile would be permanently destroyed.

Fixing a scowl to my face, I reach for the brown bag I tucked into my saddlebags. No matter how hard I try not to give in, the smile reappears instantly as I tuck the meatball hero under my arm.

When he dropped me off, there was this awkward moment where neither of us knew what to do. Then he got out of the car, leaving me still in the passenger seat. He walked around the front of the car and get this…he opened my door for me. To him it was no big deal. To me it was everything. It's true what they say, that it's the little things. The things that make you feel respected and not just wanted. Once you get a taste of that, even if it is just a small taste, you'll find yourself reevaluating your selection in men. You'll ask yourself why you ever settled for less than what you deserve, and ladies, we all deserve a man who will open our car door.

After extending a hand and helping me out of the car, Marco reached into the backseat and handed me one of the to-go bags Luigi packed for us.

If he sends you on your way with a meatball sandwich sure to make you moan, that's a bonus. If you're like me, you'll smile and without giving it much thought, you will raise the bar for yourself.

As he walked me toward my bike, I wondered if he would try to kiss me. Would I let him? Did I even want him to? Oh, who the fuck am I kidding, I totally wanted him to kiss me and I needed the kiss to be awful too.

Sloppy and rushed.

A flaw in an otherwise perfect package.

Sadly, Marco did not kiss me, so the jury is still out. Instead, he stood close and watched me straddle my bike, holding my sandwich hostage until I gave him my phone. I must've lost my mind in the last twenty-four hours because like a smitten fool, I handed him my phone. He stored his number under "Make You Moan Marco", tucked the brown bag into my saddlebag, and checked to see if my chinstrap was fastened. Tapping a finger to my nose, he told me to call him after I ate the sandwich. I was too flabbergasted to do anything but nod. He flashed me that panty-dropping grin of his and I watched as he leisurely strolled to his car. Once he was tucked into the driver's seat and out of my view, I revved my engine and the smile hasn't left my face since.

"Where the fuck were you? Your father has been waiting for over an hour."

Well that will do the trick.

Turning around, my lips settle into a thin line as Hound comes into view. Marching toward me, he flicks his cigarette into the street. The sight of him paired with the way he greeted me, really puts things into perspective. *I bet Marco doesn't talk to women like that.*

Dismissing the comparison, I stare at Hound unimpressed.

"You should really learn how to mind your business," I advise. I go to step around him, but he grabs a hold of my arm, keeping me in front of him.

"You are my business."

Tugging my arm free, I lift my eyes to his. Hound doesn't get to ruin my day. He doesn't get to wipe away the smile another man planted on my face and he certainly doesn't have the right to put his fucking hands on me.

Smacking my lips together, I point a finger at him.

"Keep your hands to yourself or you just might lose one. Not an ideal disability to have when you ride with the Corrupt Hellraisers, but I'm sure they'll find something for you to do. Maybe you can clean the clubhouse. Those rooms can get pretty dirty, especially yours. Are you still collecting condom wrappers on the floor?"

I flip my hair over my shoulder and turn my back to him. I've wasted enough time on him. Reaching the door to the clubhouse, I pull it open and step inside the smoke-filled room. It's the bewitching hour and everyone is either drunk, high, or both—a typical Tuesday for the Hellraisers. In another hour or two, this place will be full of random girls, all of them ready to drop to their knees on command.

I spot my father sitting at the end of the bar, smoking a cigar and make my way over to him. He doesn't look too pissed that I missed our dinner, but then again, my father prides himself on having a killer poker face. It's how he stays out of jail. Well, that's what he would tell you. My mother, the fancy criminal defense attorney, will say she is the reason he remains free. I guess they make a hell of a team. Too bad their coalition only works in the courtroom and the bedroom.

Sliding into the stool beside him, I lay the bag with my sandwich on the bar and reach for the bottle of whiskey sitting in front of him.

"I'm sorry I'm late," I start as I fill his shot glass. "I got tied up at work."

The lie weighs between us and guilt swarms me as I take a swig from the bottle. Too much of a coward to look at him, I keep my eyes pinned to Mouse who sits beside him rolling a blunt as thick as an Italian sausage link.

"That so?" my dad questions as he leans his beefy fore-arms on the wooden bar. Out of the corner of my eye, I watch him flick the ashes of his cigar into a red solo cup.

"Yes, but I'm here now."

Bringing the cigar back to his lips, he turns his head and studies me.

"What's in the bag?"

"Um…" my voice trails as I glance down at the bag.

"We had a dinner reservation at Il Perlino for six," he continues. "I figured it's been a while since we visited Carlo and Rosa."

Regret fills me instantly. After my mom realized parenting really wasn't her thing, she enrolled in college and left my dad alone, navigating the waters of single parenthood. Once a week, he'd leave the club behind and take me to Il Perlino for dinner. Dad would have the owners, Carlo and Rosa, sing to me if I ate my vegetables. They did a great cover of "Ti Amo" and by the time I turned ten, I could sing every word right along with them.

Once I became a teen and my dad became fully immersed in the club, our dinners at Il Perlino became less frequent. Now, we only visit our favorite restaurant on my birthday and Carlo and Rosa don't sing to me anymore. Two years ago, Rosa was diagnosed with throat cancer and had to have her larynx removed. Dad, being dad, helped Carlo keep the restaurant afloat and for one year, he paid all their bills. They were like family to us, and seeing them would've been really nice.

"It's not too late. We can still go," I suggest. Marco's meatball hero could wait until tomorrow. "Call Carlo and tell him we're on our way."

"No," Dad says. "Antonia, I'm not going to be played by my own daughter. I understand you want to live your life and to hell with me—"

"Dad—"

"Don't interrupt me," he shouts, slamming his hand against the bar. "You're so much like your mother," he adds, shaking his head. "Ironic, seeing as you can't stand her."

"I can't stand her because she left me."

"No, Antonia, she left *me*," he hisses as he shoves the cigar between his lips. It dangles from the corner of his mouth as he continues, "She wanted more from life than this." He spreads his arms wide. "She wanted to give *you* more."

Here we go again. Every time things get rough around here, my father gets in his feelings and goes on about my mother. It's nothing I haven't heard before and nothing I won't hear a million times again.

"That's why she left. It's why I funded her education. After she graduated law school and got on her feet, she came for you." He pulls the cigar from his mouth. "I can still hear the sound of her designer heels clicking across this floor," he says as he flicks his ashes. "I turned her away, Tonia. She came for you and I turned her away, told her she could be in your life, but this was your home and you belonged here with me, where I could always keep you safe."

"So she came for me," I say. "That doesn't change the script."

A mother doesn't take no for an answer when it comes to her child. Yeah, she came back and yeah, my dad refused her, but she didn't fight. She's a lawyer, it's her job to argue, and she didn't fucking fight. If she really wanted me, she would've taken him to court. She would've done everything in her power to take me away from here and give me the life she envisioned for me, but that was just an excuse. I was her out, and she fucking took it. All the hate and resentment, the phone calls I continue to ignore and visits I refuse, they are justified and no guilt trip my father dishes is going to change my mind.

"No, it doesn't," he says, curling his lip in disgust. "And the sad part is, if I had to do it all over again, I would. I'd send her fucking packing because while she may be your mother, I'm your father and a fancy law degree is going to keep you safer than me and my bare hands."

Oh, Dad, why couldn't you be a garbage man or an electrician? A postal employee or even a mechanic. A butcher! That would've been the perfect job for him.

"Dad, I'm fine. Nothing is going to happen to me."

"You don't know that," he says hoarsely. "I'm a bad man, Antonia. I've made a lot of fucking mistakes and a shit ton of enemies. I want you to live your life. I want you to have a job you love and a family…I want you to have it all, but if I let you live your life…" his voice trails and he swallows. "I don't know what I'll do if something happens to you." Turning to him, I immediately spot the tears in his eyes. "Things aren't good with the club right now. That's why I've been making you stay here and not the house. We're like a bunch of sitting ducks, just waiting for Bendetti to strike," he hisses, roughly swiping a hand over his face.

I straighten in my chair. My dad has never once dropped the name of an associate, much less a rival. Narrowing my eyes, I question him.

"Who is Bendetti?"

Realizing his mistake, he pulls his hand away from his face and quickly shakes his head, dismissing the question as he reaches for the bottle.

"It doesn't matter," he says, refilling his shot glass. I watch as he knocks back the shot with ease. Setting the glass upside down on the bar, he brings his eyes back to me.

"You like this job, yeah?"

Honestly, it's too soon to tell. I like having my independence. I like being part of the workforce. A legit one where I pay taxes, and my paycheck gets deposited directly into my bank account. Until now, any job I've had the boss is usually a guy who owes my father a favor or a dollar and pays me under the table with a little white envelope.

"I do," I admit. "The woman I work for is great and the submissions, well, I probably have enough material to write a book. You wouldn't believe half the stuff these people ask. I mean, really stupid shit and you just want to tell them to fuck off but you can't because that's not professional. Actually, I can't tell them anything because I'm an intern."

My dad's lips quirk slightly so I continue.

"It's a good steppingstone, though, and I think I can learn a lot."

"If you really want this I don't want to stand in your way, but Tonia, you can't fight me on what I'm about to say."

I suppress a groan. There's always a catch.

"Okay," I caution.

"I want you to continue to stay here until I can get a handle on this thing with the club. In the meantime, you go to work, but someone from the club follows you. They stay with you—"

"Dad, my boss doesn't know I come from a family of criminals. I can't have one of the guys sitting at a cubicle next to me."

"Fine, he can stay outside the office. You won't even know he's there."

Right, because anyone from here is going to blend in at an office.

"In the parking lot," I counter. "If I need him, I can call."

"Only if you check in throughout the day."

That seems reasonable.

"Deal! Oh, and it can't be Hound."

He narrows his eyes.

"What's the deal with you two?"

"Nothing," I lie. The last thing I need is to rehash that mess. "What about Ritmo or Mouse?" At this point I'd even take Cash or Butch, anyone but Hound.

"I'll figure it out," he replies.

"One more thing," I start, sliding off my stool. If I didn't spend time with Marco today, I probably wouldn't be adding a request. "I agreed to having a tail to and from work, but dates are off-limits."

"Tonia," he growls.

"Dad," I mock, flashing him a smile he never refuses.

Curling his lip, he shakes his head.

"No chaperones for now," he grunts. Pointing a finger at me, he narrows his eyes and continues. "But I reserve the right to change my mind. Now, go on into the kitchen. Carlo was nice enough to deliver some of your favorites and do me a favor, call your mother. She won't stop calling me because you keep ignoring her."

I start to protest, but he stands and presses a finger to my lips, silencing me.

"It's always good to have a lawyer in your back pocket."

I bet.

But it would've been good to have a mom too.

CHAPTER
ELEVEN

Marco

"I THOUGHT *JERSEY SHORE* WENT off the air," I mutter out loud as I scope out my On Demand options. Curiosity gets the best of me, so I click more info. A brief synopsis appears on the screen, revealing Snooki and company have returned for a new series and get this, Angelina is back. How's that for a little pot-stirring?

I hit play and toss the remote on the cushion beside me. Settling in, I fold my hands behind my head and prop my feet up on the coffee table.

All the girls look like they spent their earnings on plastic surgery, but my man Paulie doesn't look a day over twenty-one. It's the Italian genes, they never fail.

Feeling nostalgic, I'm about to throw my fist in the air and give it a good pump when my phone sounds with text message. Unable to tear my gaze away from the hot mess express on my television, I blindly pat the cushion beside me. Finding the phone, I flip it over and see Antonia's name on the screen.

Before we parted ways, I stored my number in her phone and sent myself a text, so I would have hers. I had given her instructions to call me after she sank her teeth into the meatball sandwich, but I didn't expect her to actually come through. She doesn't strike me as one who follows orders no matter how nicely they are delivered.

I was going to give her until eleven o'clock before I called—hence the reality tv. I needed something to get my mind off her. Something to stop me from calling and the cheap beers weren't doing the trick.

Swiping my thumb across the screen, I open her text and nearly drop the phone when I see she sent a picture of her mouth wrapped around the sandwich. Literally, it's all lips and bread.

Wait, I think that's her tongue.

Christ.

Instead of typing out a response, I tap on her contact info and hit the FaceTime icon. Fuck this texting nonsense. If she's eating, she's moaning and I don't want to just hear it, I want to experience it. I want to watch her face distort with pleasure and not that fake nonsense she pulled at the station either. I want to see her eyes roll behind her head and hear her beg for more. You know... to torture myself.

"Hold on," she says as she answers the call. There's a whole lot of camera shaking before her face finally appears on my screen and when it does, she quickly covers her mouth with her hand. "You weren't supposed to call," she says, mid-chew.

"Yeah, well, I'm not much of a dirty texter and things are about to get dirty as fuck." I tip my chin toward the screen. "Move your hand, I want to see your mouth."

Her eyes light up as she continues to chew and slowly lowers her hand from her mouth.

"That your first bite?"

She nods just before her eyelids start to close.

Here it comes.

The fucking sound I've been waiting to hear.

I sit up as she swallows, and I swear my fucking dick swells in anticipation—a sure sign I need to get laid. It's probably a good thing we left Luigi's, there was no way we were making it to the bathroom. I would've thrown her on top of the table and given the poor old man a hard attack.

Her eyes pop open and she shrugs noncommittally.

"It's good," she says finally. "I've had better."

Better, my ass.

She's full of shit.

"Take another bite," I growl, reaching for my beer with my free hand. I bring it to my lips and take a long pull as she sighs and places the phone down, giving me an aerial shot of her ceiling. A second later her face reappears.

"I had to prop the phone on something so you could see me."

She lifts the sandwich to her lips and the sight of her mouth widening hits me just as hard as the initial picture she sent. My fingers tighten around the beer, and I bite back a groan as she takes a huge bite. Dropping the sandwich onto the foil wrapper, she meets my gaze and chews.

Three...two...

A moan sounds from the back of her throat. Raspy and full of pleasure, totally worth the torture.

"You win," she says, licking her lips.

"If that was true, I'd be the one licking my lips."

Her brows furrow as I lean against the back of the sofa and take another pull from my beer.

"You didn't eat yours yet?"

I lower the bottle an inch and stare at her through the phone.

"I'm talking about eating you, Antonia, fuck the sandwich."

Her eyes widen for a split second before she quickly looks away, but there's no mistaking the tint to her cheeks. Satisfaction fills me before I press her.

"What?" I press. "Too bold?"

Tucking her hair behind her ears, a grin toys on her lips as she brings her eyes back to me.

"I can't figure you out, Pirelli," she says with a sigh, the smile still in place. "Are you a good guy or just another pig?"

"Is this a cop joke?"

"No, I'm serious. One minute you're sending me fruit—"

"Aha, so you agree it's fruit," I interrupt. The whole melon versus fruit thing was driving me insane. I had to google what the fuck a pineapple was when I got home.

She rolls her eyes and fixes me with a look.

"You opened the door for me."

Peering at her, I try to decide where she's going with this. What's wrong with opening a door for a woman? The last I checked, they dug that shit.

"So?"

"Good guys open doors for girls. Pigs play them to get laid and then leave them high and dry. If they're a real douche, they leave a sexually transmitted disease as a party favor."

Whoa.

This conversation derailed from the tracks.

"Are you telling me you have an STD?"

"God, no!" she shrieks. "I'm clean as a whistle. No party favors left here."

"Well, then are you asking me if I have one, because I don't, and I get checked every six months."

"No, I mean, that's good, but I…well…"

Then it hits me.

I sit up and place my beer bottle on the coffee table, giving my undivided attention to the pretty girl staring at me through the phone. The girl who just revealed in not so many words, she isn't as tough as she looks.

"Has no one ever held a door open for you?"

Her teeth sink into her lower lip as she lifts her eyes back to me.

Oh, girl.

Where have you been?

"I see," I say, pausing a second to find my words. I'm about to school her and send her strict no cop dating rule straight to hell.

"A guy can hold a door open for a woman, Antonia. He can walk on the curbside of the street and sit with his back to the wall and his eyes on the door while they're out to dinner. He can send her fucking gifts and call just to hear her voice. He can do all those things and still fuck her like it's his job once she's in his bed."

She releases her lip and draws in a deep breath, but I'm far from finished.

"He can talk dirty to her, tell her he wants to eat her pussy until his tongue goes numb and still be a good guy because the truth is, only a gentleman can fuck a woman properly. So he's respectful, it doesn't make him any less of a man. He'll still pull her hair and smack her ass while he bites her lips and sucks on her neck. And after he's fucked her with his mouth, he'll flip her over and pound into her like it's his God-given talent. She'll bite the pillow to keep from screaming and thank her lucky stars for the *gentleman* who made her come three times before he even thought of himself. So, yeah, I'm a good guy. I talk dirty and I fuck like a gentleman. What are you doing tomorrow night?"

That last bit comes out harsher than I intended, but my cock is about to fall off, so excuse me.

"I don't know what I'm doing tomorrow, but I know what I'm doing tonight," she mutters.

"Oh, yeah, what's that?"

My dick hardens even more against the zipper of my jeans that I lower my hand to undo the top button, hoping it gives me a little relief. It doesn't and I realize the only thing that's going to cure my throbbing cock is sticking it deep inside Antonia.

All she has to do is say the word and I'll blow every light in Brooklyn to get to her as fast as I can. Yes, I know that makes me a hypocrite, but I'm not in uniform right now and I really don't give a flying fuck.

"Masturbating."

"You going to let me watch?"

"And ruin the surprise? Never."

"Does that mean you're breaking your 'I don't date cops rule'?"

"I broke that rule the minute I decided to go to Luigi's with you."

Thank fuck for that.

"When can I see you again?" I ask her, my voice huskier than earlier.

Dragging her fingers through her hair, she hesitates.

"I know another great place. Italian too, and the chef will make you moan even louder," I say.

That earns me a chuckle.

"Oh, yeah? This place wouldn't happen to be called Pirelli's would it?"

Winking, I grin at her.

"How'd you guess?"

"I'm lucky like that," she replies. "How's Thursday?"

Thinking about my work schedule, I cringe. Richie and I are working mostly nights this week. Aside from tomorrow night, I'm not off until Saturday and while that's a perfect night for a date, I hate that I have to wait that long to get my fill of her.

"I'm working nights this week. How about Saturday?"

"That works," she says. "Text me your address."

"Why don't you do all New Yorkers a favor and stay off the road. I'll pick you up around seven."

She shakes her head.

"No, that won't work."

"Why not, I know where you live, remember?"

"You know on second thought, Saturday isn't good."

"Antonia…"

"Monday," she suggests. "After work, I can come to you."

I don't know if she's trying to hide something from me or if she's got an issue with surrendering control, but the girl is hell-bent on meeting me and I don't like it. If it's a control thing, we're going to have to kick that habit real quick. When we finally fuck I'll be the one controlling the show.

"I'll pick you up from the office," I tell her. "Oh, and take the subway to work, Antonia, you'll be spending the night at my place."

"Is that so?"

I nod.

"And because I'm a gentleman, I'll make you breakfast in the morning."

"Before or after you eat me?"

Now, she's getting it.

"After of course."

Always after.

CHAPTER TWELVE

Marco

"Pay up, Pirelli," Judy says, shoving her open palm in my face.

Flashing her a smile, I lean back in my chair.

"Is it Friday already?"

Every two weeks a couple of us pool our money together and buy a bunch of lotto tickets. We've hit a couple of numbers here and there, but nothing life-changing. I think at this point we do it just to keep Judy happy. The broad loves to take our money.

Lifting my hips off the seat of the chair, I dig into my pocket and pull out some cash. The smile falls from my face when I notice I only have large bills.

"I only have a fifty," I tell her.

She plucks it from my fingers.

"I'll bring you change."

She walks away before I can object, not that I would. She can keep the fifty bucks if it keeps her off my back.

Turning my attention back to my screen, I crack my fingers and attack the keyboard, typing the Corrupt Hellraisers into the search engine of our database. I told myself I wasn't going to do it, that whatever Antonia had going on with that guy Hound was no business of mine. But after spending the last three days talking and texting, something just doesn't add up.

The first clue came when she dodged any attempt I made to pick her up for our date. I shrugged it off and decided it was nothing out of the norm. There are plenty of girls who prefer to drive themselves, especially when things are new. No judgments here, and not because I won that battle. If I really believed she was more comfortable driving herself, I would have relented. But Antonia wasn't throwing off that vibe. She wanted a man to pick her up and hold doors for her. Hell, I think she craved it more than anything.

The night before last, while we were on the phone, someone came into her bedroom. She muted the call and when she returned, she quickly hung up, using the excuse she had to walk her dog. The night before she told me she didn't have any pets. She had a fish once, though. Petey was his name, and he died after she tried to feed him a cannoli. So, she definitely wasn't walking him.

I called her back a little while later and she sent my call straight to voicemail. I woke up the next morning to a text. It was a picture of her tits covered in a red lace bra and like a horny teenager, I forgot all about the fake pet.

But this morning my suspicions were confirmed when I stopped by her office on my way home from work. Something wasn't kosher, and it wasn't the bagel and lox I decided to bring her for breakfast. It was the fucking guy with the leather vest tailing her. My first thought was that it was Hound, but once I pulled my car into the garage, I got a better look at the guy. He wasn't quite as tall as the fuck who punched me in the face and where Hound's arms were the only visible part of his body with any tattoos, this dude had ink crawling up his neck. He also had two teardrops tattooed beneath his left eye—a calling card that told me he either took two lives in prison or was fronting like he did.

Now, I don't know much about motorcycle clubs, but I know the basics. A prospect must prove his worth before he receives his patch. I'm guessing two bodies would prove a man worthy or at least put him in the running.

Instead of making my presence known, I left the scene and took my ass home. I had barely known Antonia a week, and I decided I had long crossed the point of no return where she was concerned. I was fully invested, and not just for the sake of fucking her. The more we spoke, the more I found myself wanting to know everything about her and without even realizing it, I was becoming protective over her. Crazy, considering we barely had one date.

Before I get in any deeper with her, I need to uncover whatever it is she's trying to hide from me. I need to know if Hound is more than just a piece of her past and what her connection is to all these fucking bikers. For fuck's sake, one of them is a self-proclaimed murderer. What if she's in some kind of trouble?

That last question weighs heavily on me as I click search.

As a cop, it's my duty to protect, but Antonia isn't official police business, she's just a girl I'm dating. A girl I was supposed to take to bed and forget. Now, I'm doing background checks on gangbangers and looking up recipes for chicken piccata because she mentioned it's her favorite. How we got here, I'm not sure. All I know for certain is this isn't the normal behavior for Marco Pirelli.

The computer screen loads with the information, and I

lean over my desk to get a better look. There are mugshots, arrest records, and a fucking family tree on the ranking of every member, but only one name stands out.

Antonio DeLuca.

Or more commonly known as Tank Deluca.

I click on his file, and his face immediately fills the screen. Eyes that resemble Antonia's stare back at me. Only where hers are full of fire, his are cold and menacing. I continue to scroll and discover the man is the president of the Corrupt Hellraiser's Brooklyn charter. He's also Antonia's father, and he has had a shit ton of charges put out on him.

Drug trafficking.

Attempted murder.

Possession of firearms with intent to sell.

Prostitution.

Money laundering.

You fucking name it and this guy has been charged with it, but from the looks of it, nothing sticks.

Forget O.J. Simpson, whoever DeLuca has on retainer is the real dream team.

I keep scrolling, bypassing all the arrests and the list of criminals he's been linked to and freeze when I spot the one charge that actually did stick. Thirty years ago, DeLuca did a bid for aggravated assault on a cop. He had no priors at the time, so he was out in five years. That should be a crime in itself, yet all it appears to be is the beginning of DeLuca's affair with breaking the law.

It's no wonder his daughter doesn't date cops.

The question is, now that I know who her father is, what the fuck am I going to do with her?

"Pirelli!" Judy shouts, tearing my attention away from the screen. "Here's your change," she says, throwing a twenty at me. "I bought myself a cup of coffee and a danish too."

PULLING THE BEER BOTTLE AWAY from my lips, I glare at my cousin, Tig, as he continues to ignore my rant.

"Did you not hear a word I just said? Her father is a fucking convicted felon."

He pauses with the tattoo gun in his hand and lifts his eyes from his client's back.

"So?"

"So, I'm a cop!"

Sighing, Tig takes his foot off the pedal, powering down the gun. The buzzing sound dies, and he pats his client on the shoulder.

"Gary, give me a minute," he says, pulling the rubber gloves from his hands.

"Sure, bro," Gary replies. "I'm going to go out for a smoke." He pauses in front of me and shakes his head before glancing back at Tig. "Good luck with this one."

This coming from a guy who is tattooing a tarantula to his back. When Gary is out of sight, I turn back to Tig.

"Your client is an asshole."

"Same could be said about you."

I bring the beer back to my lips and take another long pull.

"You've been going on about this girl for a week," he points out.

"Six days," I correct.

"Soraya says you sent her a fruit basket and took her to Luigi's," he pauses, crossing his arms against his chest. "You took the girl to your favorite restaurant, seems like a big deal to me."

Lowering my beer, I raise an eyebrow.

"Good to know you and Soraya have nothing better to talk about," I mutter. Dropping my eyes to the bottle in my hand, I start to pick at the label. "You're no fucking help."

"You don't need my help," he says. "You need to pull your head out of your ass. You're not dating her father, you're dating her."

"I hate that word."

"Dating?" he questions.

"Yeah," I admit. "All I wanted was to get her out of my system. One fucking night."

Tig laughs, and my gaze snaps back to him.

"It's not funny," I argue. "I don't know what I'm doing. She's not like any other girl I've met before. She's a firecracker wrapped in leather, with wild hair and beautiful eyes. Complete with a smart mouth and a fucking ass you just want to sink your teeth into."

She's every man's perfect fantasy, but she's my reality.

Or at the very least, she could've been.

"She comes off like she's tough as nails and at first glance, you think a man can't break her. That she chews them up and spits them out when she's had her fill. But the more you learn about her, the more you realize under all that leather there is just a girl. No one's held a door for her, Tig. No fucking man has ever shown her that simple respect."

"I'm not really sure where you're going with this," he says. "I think you want to hold her door open for her, am I right? She's got a great ass and you want to hold doors for her, that's gotta be it."

"Yeah, I want to hold her door. I want her to know there are guys out there who recognize her worth and respect her. Maybe then she'll stop dating fucking felons like Hound."

"Okay, so what's the problem? Take her out, show her a good time and see where it goes."

"It can't go anywhere."

"Because you and her daddy play on opposite sides of the law? Who gives a fuck? You aren't building a case against the man. You're fucking his daughter."

"I'm not fucking her," I hiss.

"Well, that's just ignorant. What are you waiting for?"

I was waiting for Monday and Chicken Piccata.

"She hasn't told me who her father is," I tell him. "There's a reason she doesn't want me to know and my guess is, it has a lot to do with him doing time for assaulting an officer."

Sighing, he leans forward and braces his elbows on his knees.

"Let me ask you a question, do you plan on telling her you know the truth about her old man?"

And confess to doing a search on the Corrupt Hellraisers? Is he crazy?

"Fuck, no."

"Then unless you plan on proposing sometime soon, just go with the flow."

"Bite your tongue."

Laughing, he swipes a hand over his face.

"Man, I give you six months before you're asking me to go ring shopping with you."

"You're out of your mind," I scoff.

Fucking insane is what he is.

"Make it three months."

He stands and grabs a fresh pair of rubber gloves.

"Now, if you're done PMSing, I got work to do."

"I'm your next client," I tell him, taking another swig of my beer.

"The fuck you are. Make an appointment and see to it you're not drunk when you do. I don't need you bleeding like a pig in my chair."

He's gotta be kidding me. I've been waiting four weeks for him to finish the piece on my back.

"Oh, come on. It's just a beer. You make it like I swallowed a bottle of Heparin."

"Make an appointment," he repeats.

"I'll just ask Delia to finish it."

His eyes slice back to me.

"Leave Delia alone," he grinds out.

The tone of his voice sobers me up some and I sit straighter in my chair. I'm such a dick. All this time I've been sitting here, wallowing in my misery when he and Delia are living a nightmare of their own.

"Everything okay?"

He looks away.

"No, but what's the use in complaining about it? Ain't gonna change a damn thing. I can't give her what she wants…what we both want. I got the debt and an empty nursery to prove it."

"I'm sorry, man," I empathize.

I wish there was more I could say, but there are no right words when it comes to their situation. Do you pray for them? It seems rather pointless when all their prayers go unanswered. Soraya is sure this party we're planning will bring them some joy, but what happens when they wake up the next morning and the pain they forgot for a couple of hours is still there?

Sighing, Tig shakes his head.

"It is what it is. I'm going to go get Gary so I can finish his session. You good to drive home?"

"Yeah."

He nods and starts for the front door. Pausing midway, he turns and looks at me.

"Hey," he calls.

"Yeah?"

"I want to meet her."

"Who?"

"Your girl," he clarifies. "I want to meet her. Delia and I can use a night out and I can't think of a better way to spend our time than watching you act like a lovesick fool. Set it up."

With that, he turns on his heel.

My mouth drops open to say something, but I quickly smack my lips together.

Looks like I just got them to the party, and I didn't even have to lift a finger or concoct some crazy story.

Who's better than me?

CHAPTER THIRTEEN

ANTONIA

THE WEEKEND PASSED WITHOUT MUCH contact from Marco, odd considering how much we spoke from Tuesday to Friday. If we weren't texting, we were FaceTiming, and we didn't go more than two hours without hearing from one another. Friday afternoon I called him, and he rushed me off the phone. I figured the back to back night shifts were getting to him. Either that or he had a secret wife and child he was trying to hide. Dramatic, I know, especially considering I was the one hiding a family of bikers.

Saturday he was off and told me he planned on catching up on his sleep before heading to his cousin's tattoo shop, so I didn't call him at all. Sunday morning, he texted me, but again it was brief which only fueled my paranoia more.

You can imagine how miserable I was all day, thinking he was going to ghost me for our date. I spent most of my lunch hour plotting how I'd get back at him for making a fool out of me. Five o'clock came and there was still no word from him.

Still, I called my father and told him I had a date and ordered him to call off my tail as per our agreement. I pulled my bag over my shoulder and shut down my computer. On my way to the elevator, I realized if Marco didn't show, I was going to have to ride the subway back home. Once, this morning was enough. That thing was a cesspool of germs—another strike for Marco Pirelli.

I pressed the button for the elevator and when the doors opened, there he stood with a sexy smile on his face. Soraya had already left for the day, so he didn't exit to greet his friend and he didn't pay any mind to Penelope who was lurking behind me. Instead, he reached for me and pulled me inside the elevator, pressing his lips to my cheek. They were soft and cool against my heated skin, and I yearned to feel them against mine. He didn't let on that something was wrong and before I knew it, the anger I felt and all the crazy suspicions I had before he arrived, disappeared.

Just like Tuesday, he opened the car door for me and when we entered his apartment complex, he waited for me to step onto the elevator first.

"Ladies first," he whispered against my ear.

I turned my head, and he winked at me. If there was any chance of me ending this night with my panties on, it officially went out the window. Apparently, I was a sucker for a good guy. I'm sorry, correction, a good guy with a filthy mouth who prided himself on being a gentleman in the bedroom.

His words, not mine.

Anyway, this newfound type of mine was going to take some time getting used to, something I realized once we were in his apartment and I discovered he was cooking one of my all-time favorite dishes. I've always thought dating the bad boy was fun and exciting. Sure, it left me with a broken heart most of the time, but I held onto hope that there would eventually be one guy who was more broken than bad and with any luck, I'd be the girl who changed him. The girl who made him want to be better.

But what if dating all those bad boys and suffering all that heartbreak was for a greater purpose? What if I needed to choose a man who would hurt me to be able to recognize one who wouldn't?

It's too soon to tell if Marco is that guy, but until now I never really thought about any of this.

Now, I'm sitting on a barstool at the kitchen island, eating capers from a jar, watching him work his magic and besides wondering if he's the one guy who won't hurt me, I'm also pondering if he's as skillful in the bedroom as he is behind the stove.

"Refill?" he asks, eyeing my empty wineglass. I tear my attention away from the jar of capers I've been picking on and meet his gaze.

He even bought my favorite brand of Pinot Grigio when I assured him, I was fine with beer.

Pushing my wineglass toward him, I smile.

"Are you trying to get me drunk?"

He shakes his head as he pours the wine.

"I want you relaxed and fully coherent for dessert."

"Is this the part where I ask what's for dessert and you come back with some comment full of sexual innuendo?"

He finishes topping off my glass and sets the bottle of wine on the granite surface. Bracing his hands on the edge of the counter, he leans forward and his gaze dips toward my mouth.

"Is it really innuendo if we both already know you *are* what's for dessert?"

"That's all fine and good for you, but what about me?"

His grin widens, and a wicked gleam appears in his eyes. "I'll let you have a taste too."

Christ, he's sexy and with very little effort. It just comes naturally to him.

Exhaling roughly, I trace the rim of the wineglass with the tip of my finger and peer up at him from beneath the fringe of my lashes before asking, "Because you aim to please?"

He reaches out and touches a finger under my chin. Our eyes lock as his thumb glides to my lips.

"Exactly," he says huskily.

I almost ask him if we can forget dinner altogether, but the pot with the rice boils over, breaking our trance. His hand drops away from my face and he mutters a curse. Turning back to the stove, he lowers the flame under the pot, and I take a long drink of wine. My entire body feels heated and I decide to steer the conversation away from sex.

"So, I met Soraya's husband today," I begin, watching as he bends to check the chicken in the oven. There's something so sexy about a man who can cook.

"Oh, yeah, how's Graham doing these days?"

"I don't know, I didn't pay him too much mind. As soon as Soraya introduced us, I imagined his head as a dartboard and envisioned myself throwing darts at him because he punched you."

Straightening up, he barks out a laugh.

"You know you don't have to win me over, Curly Sue. I'm already yours and I'm set to deliver on all the orgasms I promised you."

"I'm being serious," I argue. Tearing my eyes away from him, I shove my spoon back into the jar of capers. "Eventually I realized I was being ridiculous and ordered myself to stop judging him based on an argument he had with you long before I even met you." I pause to eat another spoonful of capers. Thoughtfully, I continue, "You know, at first glance, you look at him and Soraya and wonder how they fell for one another."

She's such a free spirit, and he's this proper package wrapped in a suit. She looks the type to break the rules, and he looks like the type to enforce them. It must make for a whole lot of fun in the bedroom.

Shit, that's weird.

I've officially sunk to a new low when I start wondering about my boss's sex life.

Shaking my head, I shrug my shoulders and look back at Marco.

"I guess it's true opposites attract. Anyway, you and Graham are good now?"

"Yeah, we're cool. You can stop pretending to throw darts at his head," he teases. There's a glint of amusement in his eyes as he leans his back against the counter and reaches for his beer. "I don't see him all that much," he continues, pausing. "To be fair, until a couple of weeks ago, I hadn't seen much of Soraya either."

I find that surprising. When he came to take her to lunch, they seemed as though they were best friends who saw each other all the time.

"What changed?"

The bottle stills at his lips, and he frowns slightly. Setting the beer on the counter, he sighs and looks back at me.

"Remember I told you about my cousin Tig?"

"The guy who owns the tattoo shop?"

"Yeah, he and his wife Delia are coming up on their tenth wedding anniversary and for the last couple of years, they've been trying to conceive. It has been one hurdle after another for them, and they just recently decided to throw in the towel. Not an easy decision for either of them, but I guess you gotta know when to fold."

"Did they go to infertility a specialist?"

He nods.

"They put every dime they had into trying to have a baby and exhausted several treatments and procedures. Tig used to have to give her hormone shots. I remember one day I walked into the shop and Delia was crying because he was about to poke her with a big ass needle. Tig teased her, after all, needles and ink are their bread and butter." He pauses to shake his head. "Anyway, when that didn't work, they took a mortgage out on the shop for IVF. The first two times they did it, it didn't take and they're tapped out on cash to try for a third round. Graham offered them a loan, but Tig would rather roll over and die before he takes a handout from anyone. It's crazy, you know? Tig is a scary motherfucker. Fearless. He isn't the type to show weakness or break."

"Everybody breaks," I whisper.

He brings his eyes back to me and stares at me thoughtfully for a moment before nodding in agreement.

"Yeah, I guess they do."

Listening to Marco talk about his cousins made me want to meet them. Hell, I wanted to hug them. Picture wanting something so badly and doing everything you can to make it happen only to be told you're shit out of luck. Then magnify those feelings by ten. It makes you question everything, but most of all your faith.

"What about adoption?" I ask.

"They're looking into it, but it's not easy. There's a lot of red tape to cut through, never mind the horror stories you hear. Like the birth mother deciding she wants to keep the kid after it's born and stuff like that." He sighs. "I don't know that they're mentally prepared for that just yet. If something went wrong, I think that would just throw them over the edge."

I didn't know what to say. Until you walk a mile in someone else's shoes, I'm not sure you're entitled to have an opinion on their life. All you can do is offer your support, and it seems like Marco is team Tig and Delia all the way. Another admirable quality for the good cop.

"Sorry, I guess I put a damper on tonight with the heavy stuff. I don't know why I told you all that."

"I asked you how you and Soraya started to speak," I supply, rising from the stool. Rounding the island, I grab the dishes and utensils from the counter and start to set the little table.

"Right, well, Soraya thought it would be a good idea to throw them an anniversary party. She thinks it'll take their minds off things and lift their spirits." He shrugs. "I don't know if it will work, but I'm all in. Whatever they need."

He comes to stand behind me and touches his hands to my hips. I stop setting the table and turn around to face him.

"I told Tig about you," he says, tucking a strand of hair behind ear.

I don't know why that makes my stomach flutter.

"You did?"

He nods.

"He wants to meet you."

No one's ever taken me home to meet the family. Not a mother, or a father. No siblings and no cousins.

"Why?" I stammer.

"Probably because I couldn't stop talking about you on Saturday," he replies, smiling at me. "The party is next week, and Soraya appointed me the guy responsible for getting them there. It's a surprise, so my options are limited, and your boss is no help."

"You want to take me to a family party?"

"It's not really a family party, we just invited their

friends. Tig and Delia aren't likely to close the shop for no good reason when they're swimming in debt, but if I dangled you in front of them, well, you're pretty irresistible. So, what do you say?"

"I don't know. That would mean another week of talking to you and I'm not really in the market for a long-term relationship," I tease, a big fat grin spreading across my lips. Lifting my arms, I wind them around his neck. "I'd love to go with you."

"Then it's settled," he rasps, bringing his hands back to my hips. Our noses brush as he pulls in a deep breath. "I planned on waiting until after dinner."

"For what?"

"This."

He lowers his head, and his lips brush with mine. It's slow at first, almost teasing but then his tongue rolls over my bottom lip and I welcome him into my mouth. My arms tighten around his neck and his fingers dig into my hips as I fall against his hard body.

A moan sounds from the back of his throat as his teeth playfully nip at my lower lip. Spinning us around, he moves me away from the table and pushes me against the wall. His hand comes up to my neck, curling around the back of it, holding me in place as his lips continue to attack mine. Heat pools between my legs as his tongue rolls over mine and I inch even closer. His erection presses against my belly and it's my turn to moan.

Fuck.

I really needed him to be an awful kisser.

The timer on the oven goes off and Marco slowly tears his mouth away from mine, peppering my lips with chaste kisses.

"Dinner's ready," he rasps, meeting my hooded gaze.

Screw the chicken, give me more of that.

CHAPTER
FOURTEEN

Marco

Earlier, I decided I was going to take Tig's advice and just go with the flow. I wasn't going to worry about who Antonia's father was or why she was keeping it from me. And I wasn't going to mention the fucking creep hanging around outside the office or that sleazeball Hound either. I was simply going to enjoy her, and by that, I mean, I was going to give us both a night we'd never forget.

All that other stuff would come with time.

With trust.

But when she agreed to come to the party with me, something inside me snapped. I can't explain it, but I needed to taste her. It's been twenty minutes since my mouth touched hers and I'm still fucking hard as a rock. I could give a fuck less about the chicken on my plate. All I've got is an appetite for her.

"You've barely touched your food."

Reaching for my beer, I twist the top off and glance at my dish before meeting Antonia's gaze.

Christ, she's pretty.

"That's because I'm currently wondering if your pussy tastes as sweet as your mouth and it's taking every ounce of self-control not to flip this table and pull your leather pants down."

Watching as her cheeks flame, I bring the bottle to my lips and take a gulp. My imagination kicks into gear and I picture her sprawled across my bed, her cheeks flush, her hair mussed and sweat dripping from her brow.

"Oh," she murmurs, setting her fork down. It's not a graceful move, and it hits the dish with a clank. Her tongue slips over her bottom lip slowly, enticing me. Driving me fucking mad. Then she pulls it between her teeth, and I'm done. Just fucking done.

Lowering my hand under the table, I press the heel of my hand to the bulge between my legs and reach for my fork. Stabbing the chicken with the prongs of the fork, I close my eyes and try to picture something unattractive. Something sure to kill the party in my pants.

My Nonna comes to mind.

My sweet, loving and very dead, Nonna.

May she rest in peace.

"We could skip dinner," Antonia says as I pop a piece of chicken into my mouth.

As tempting as that is, I shake my head. I'm not a horny teenager who can't control himself. I'm a fucking man and I don't want to be another name on the list of douchebags she's dated. For some odd reason, I want her to place me in a category of my own.

Meeting her gaze, I say, "I'm going to school you on something. If a man can't get his dick under control and sit through a meal with a beautiful woman, he's going to be selfish in the bedroom. It's all about patience."

"Let me guess, you're patient."

"In not so many words you just gave me the green light to fuck you and we're still sitting at the table. What do you think?"

"I think you better live up to the expectations you're making me have."

I laugh, cutting another piece of chicken.

"I'll try my best," I retort, winking at her.

Determined to make it through the meal, I shifted our conversation. Instead of talking about her lips and how perfect they would look wrapped around my cock or how badly I wanted to bury my face between her tits, we took the time to get to know one another better. We had been doing a lot of that during the week over the phone, but she's always the one asking the questions. The girl could write a book on me and all I know about her are half-truths.

I got myself another beer, poured her another glass of wine, and started with the small stuff. One question bled into four and I learned once Antonia loosened up, she liked to talk.

She told me a little about her mom, and how they didn't get along, but didn't elaborate on why. Antonia liked to talk, but she was very elusive with information. She gave you bits and pieces of a story and watched you intently as she spoke. It was almost as if she was waiting for a reaction, for someone to judge her for whatever it was she was sharing. If you smiled at her, she would continue revealing another fact, but if you showed the slightest bit of concern or asked for more information, she quickly changed the subject. She was a tricky one to figure out, and I was learning there were many layers to Antonia DeLuca, layers she had yet to discover herself. Layers she buried. I wanted to peel back every single one and I would with time because with time came trust.

The conversation tapered off after a while and we cleared the table. Rolling up my sleeves, I got to work on the dishes. Antonia insisted on helping despite my best efforts and hoisted herself onto the counter next to the sink. We had a nice system. I washed, she dried, and we continued talking, taking turns on who asked questions.

"That's the last one," I say, turning off the tap.

Leaning my hip against the sink, I cross my arms and study her as she finishes drying the last plate.

"You're staring, Pirelli," she points out, gently setting the dry dish on top of the others.

"You're only noticing now? I've been staring at you all night."

Kicking off the cabinet, I make my way toward her. She folds the dishtowel and sets it on the counter next to her as my hands move to her knees, gently coaxing them apart. I step between them and lift my hands to cup her cheeks. She lifts her chin, and her eyes find mine. There's a glint of mischief there, and a plea too.

"I got you something," I tell her.

Her eyes light up at that and I decide watching her react to me might be my new favorite pastime.

"Is it another bouquet of melon?"

Laughing, I lean forward and kiss the side of her mouth. My hands fall from her face and take purchase on her thighs, giving them a squeeze as my lips trail toward her jaw.

I should stop.

Put on a movie.

Maybe some music.

Take her for a fucking walk.

Something.

"Mmm…" she moans, tightening her legs around me. Her arms snake around me, and she curls her fingers into my shirt. If I don't pull back now, this is going to escalate quicker than I planned. My teeth nip at the underside of her jaw for another second before I peel my mouth away and her eyes flutter open instantly.

"Why'd you stop?"

I reach over her thigh and pull open the drawer next to her, taking out a small paper bag. She eyes it curiously as I hand it to her.

"Open it," I urge.

She takes the bag and I drop my hands to her thighs. I watch as she peeks into the bag. A laugh rolls from her lips as she lifts her eyes back to mine.

"You bought me a lightbulb?"

"Hey, that's not just any old lightbulb, it's a replacement bulb for the taillight on your bike. When I take you home, I'll swap it out for you. You don't need any pain in the ass cops pulling you over and giving you a ticket for a simple fix."

"I thought we decided I was spending the night?"

"Yeah, but I figured you'd want me to drive you home before work."

"I brought clothes and a toothbrush. If it's not too much trouble, you can just drop me off at the office."

I forgot about that and suddenly it makes sense why she was so adamant about me picking her up from work. She didn't want me anywhere near her house. I decide not to make a big deal of it.

Trust.

She just needs to be able to trust you.

Give her time.

Biting the inside of my cheek, I give her a nod.

"Right, sure, just make sure you change it out. Wouldn't want another cop pulling you over."

She brings her hand to the front of my tee and pulls me closer.

"Thank you," she whispers before closing her mouth over mine.

Her mouth opens invitingly, and I slip my tongue inside, tasting the wine on hers. My mind goes blank and I get drunk on the taste of her. With each flick of my tongue, she grows impatient, and soon her legs are locked around my back and I find myself carrying her away from the kitchen.

In my bedroom, I deposit her on the foot of my bed and tear my mouth away from hers. I drop to my knees between her legs and lift one leg, finding the zipper of her boot. Dragging it down, I pull the leather from her calf and chuck the boot over my head. She giggles softly and runs her fingers through my hair, pulling me back to her lips.

I forget about the second boot and raise my hands, fisting her hair between my fingers as I pry her lips apart with my tongue. The scent of her perfume fills my nostrils and a daunting thought crosses my mind. This room will never be the same. The scent of her will be on my sheets and I'm not even bothered by it.

Her hands slip under my shirt and travel up my chest.

"Take it off," she hisses against my lips.

I break the kiss to pull my shirt over my head and her eyes instantly drop, taking me in from the waistband of my jeans all the way up. Muttering something in Italian, she lunges for me, winding her arms around my neck. Our lips collide again in a frantic rush. Her nails dig into the flesh at the back of my neck and I bend my head to suck on hers.

"Yes," she moans. "I love that."

I tease her with my mouth, leaving my mark on her olive skin and bring my hand to her breast, squeezing her through the fabric of her t-shirt. I can feel her pert nipple and I roll my thumb over it as my teeth graze her collarbone.

Her breath hitches as I pull away.

"No, don't stop," she begs.

"You're wearing entirely too many clothes."

"Let's fix that," she pants, lifting the hem of her t-shirt. My mouth waters and my dick grows with every inch of skin she exposes. Her black lace bra comes in to view and I'm rendered speechless. She tosses the shirt to the side and reaches behind her to unclasp her bra. The cups loosen and she brings her arms back around, slowly lowering one strap from her shoulder, then the other.

"Fuck," I rasp the second the bra falls to her lap.

Pulling her lower lip between her teeth, she uncrosses her arms and drops them to her side, revealing the most perfect pair of tits I've ever seen. I swallow hard as I drink her in, those pert nipples calling for my mouth.

Tearing my eyes away from them, I make work of her other boot. I lift both her legs and wind them around my waist. I take one breast in my hand, rolling my thumb over her nipple.

"You're fucking perfect," I tell her, giving her other tit a firm squeeze. "So goddamn perfect."

She moans in response, and I bend my head, opening my mouth around her nipple. Sucking it, I use my tongue and teeth to taunt her. She arches against me, those leather pants sticking to my slick skin as I flick my tongue over her nipple. She cries out as I move to the other one, inflicting the same sweet torture on it. Between the scruff on my face and my teeth, her tits are red by the time I finally come up for air.

I take her mouth again, kissing her hard as I lower her back onto the mattress. Detangling her legs from my waist, I spread them apart. Peeling the leather from her legs is going to be a job in itself, but I'm up for the challenge and what a fucking beautiful challenge it is.

Standing up, I take a step forward. My knees touch the end of the mattress as I lean over her and slip my fingers under the elastic band of her pants.

"Lift your hips," I order.

Fisting my comforter, she arches her body. Her ass lifts off the mattress as I start to peel the leather away, exposing the skimpy scrap of lace covering the sweetest part of her.

"Christ," I rasp, forcing myself to focus on the task at hand. Once I've got the pants off, I push her legs further apart and bring two fingers to her lace covered pussy.

"You're soaking wet," I say, sliding my fingers up and down her slit, her arousal coating them. Instead of licking them clean like I want to, I lift my eyes to hers.

"How attached to these panties are you?"

"Why?" she pants.

"I'm about to destroy them."

I don't give her a chance to respond and slip my fingers under the lace, tearing them to the side with a forceful tug. The lace rips as I drop back to my knees and smash my mouth against her bare pussy. I lick her slowly, flicking my tongue against her clit.

"Fuck yes," she cries as I lift her legs over my shoulders. Gripping her ass cheeks, I pull her toward my mouth. In and out, I slide my tongue deeper and deeper until her hips buck and she's riding my tongue, chasing a high she's desperate to feel.

Before she peaks, I pull away and right her panties. Ripped and all, I use the lace as friction and bring my fingers back to her clit, rubbing it in slow motions.

"You're killing me, Pirelli," she whimpers. "Give me your mouth again, I was almost there."

"Not yet."

"But…"

"Spread your legs wider," I growl, removing my fingers. I finally give in and bring them to my mouth, sucking them clean. The taste of her explodes on my tongue. If I could bury myself between her legs and feast on her every day for the rest of my life, I'd die a happy man.

"Marco."

I shake my head, releasing my fingers with a pop. My hand falls to the waistband of my jeans as my eyes lock with hers.

I can't fucking take it anymore.

"Wider, Antonia," I order, popping the button on my jeans. Dragging the denim down my legs, I kick them aside and grab my cock through my boxers, watching as her heels dig into my mattress as she widens her stance. Her hand moves between her legs, and she pushes the torn lace aside. Keeping her eyes pinned to mine, she inserts two fingers into her pussy.

"If you're not going to…"

"Take your fingers out," I growl.

"But."

"Take your fucking fingers out of your pussy, Antonia."

She does, and my hand closes around her wrist. Dragging her fingers to my mouth, I suck on them. Her breath hitches as I pull them from my mouth and press them to hers.

"Open for me, dollface." Without hesitating, her lips part and I shove my fingers into her mouth. "Thatta girl," I whisper, watching as her cheeks hollow out and she sucks on them.

She's going to look so good with my cock in her mouth.

So fucking good.

Patience, man.

It will kill you.

Fucking wreck you.

Her tongue swirls around my fingers as I slowly draw them out of her mouth.

"God, you're a sight," I rasp.

A beautiful fucking sight.

Her fingers move to my boxers and close around my cock.

"Please," she begs. "I can't wait any longer."

"Tell me what you want."

"Isn't it obvious?" she questions, cupping my balls through the black fabric.

"I'm not done with you," I argue, taking her nipple between my teeth.

"You proved your point."

"Did I?" I say against her breast.

"Yes," she cries, lowering my boxers until my cock springs free. Her fingers close around my shaft, and my mouth stills around her nipple. Closing my eyes, I let myself revel in her touch for a moment before I cover her hand with mine, guiding it up and down my shaft before pushing her away.

"Marco."

"Flip over," I demand, shucking the boxers down my legs. Like my jeans, I kick them off. Her brows furrow as she stares back at me. "On all fours, Antonia. Now."

Her eyes light with excitement and I watch as she rolls over, giving me a spectacular view of her ass. I jerk my cock as she moves into position, her knees and palms working to lift her body off the mattress.

Pulling my hand away from my shaft, I climb on the bed behind her. I slide my hands between her legs and push them apart. Fitting my head there, I drop my back to the mattress. My hands curl around her thighs. She looks down at me. Eyes locked, I swipe my tongue over the lace.

"You want to come?" I ask.

She nods and I move her panties aside once more.

"Then fuck my face until you come, beautiful."

CHAPTER
FIFTEEN

ANTONIA

MARCO DOESN'T HAVE TO SAY it twice. I lower myself onto his waiting mouth, wrap my fingers tightly around the wrought iron bars of his headboard, and rock slowly against his tongue. Being on top allows me to chase my orgasm without interruption. He can't tease me anymore and he can't bring me to the tip of the crest to steal my pleasure. I'm the one in control and I love it.

The scruff of his five o'clock shadow.

His playful nips.

The languid strokes of his tongue and pressure against my clit.

It's everything.

The faster I ride him, the more frantic I become. Every sensitive nerve comes alive, and it feels like fireworks are going off inside of my body. I try to slow down, to savor the sensation, but I can't. I'm at the mercy of my pleasure.

Marco must sense this because, in one sudden move, his

hands slide from the back of my thighs up to my hips. He pulls me down with such force, my knees give out and I find myself actually sitting on his face. My body surrenders to his mouth and I come fast and hard, pleasure ripping through my body with a violent force.

When it seems impossible for me to take another stroke of his tongue, he lifts me off his mouth and rolls me onto my back. My eyes fight for focus as my gaze finds his handsome face. Licking his lips devilishly, he reaches for a condom and tears the foil packet open with his teeth.

Trying to catch my breath, I watch as he rolls it on his thick shaft. Sheathed, he fists his cock for a second before taking my arms and pinning them over my head.

My hair, damp from sweat and a matted mess, sticks to my face. I go to tuck it behind my ears so I can get a better look at him when he enters me, but his hold on my hands tighten.

"Keep your hands above your head and your body still," he demands roughly.

My lips part in protest, but he shakes his head and gives my wrists another squeeze. Bringing one hand to my face, he gently brushes the hair away from my eyes. His other hand joins in the task and I struggle to keep my arms over my head as requested. A whimper escapes the back of my throat as he combs his fingers through my curls, giving them a hard pull. Growling, he fans my curls over the pillow and meets my gaze.

"Better," he murmurs before lowering his head and taking my mouth. I'm not sure where he gets his patience or his stamina from. Until tonight a part of me wondered if he was all smoke and mirrors, but the man has every right to be as cocky as he is when it comes to sex. If this is what it's like being fucked by a gentleman, well, sign me up for seconds... and thirds.

"You're so fucking beautiful when you come," he says against my mouth.

He sucks my lower lip between his teeth before releasing it and peppering kisses down the smooth column of my neck. It becomes increasingly harder to keep my hands off him, especially when he grabs my hips and gets on his knees between my legs. Pulling me closer, he positions the head of his cock at my entrance. Closing my eyes, I bite the inside of my cheek and wait to feel him inside of me.

"Antonia, give me your eyes," he orders.

Looking at him as he fills me makes me feel very vulnerable. My eyes are like a piece of glass, a window to every emotion. I can't hide behind the tough girl façade. Every feeling and every thought are all on display for him. It's very intimate and equally terrifying.

"Thatta' girl," he praises, dipping his head to touch his forehead to mine. He slides into me, inch by inch, stretching me until I'm fully impaled. "God, you feel amazing," he murmurs as he begins to move.

In and out.

Slow and steady.

The sound of his skin slapping against mine fills my ears and the scent of sex assaults my senses. I realize this is like nothing I have ever experienced before and when he picks up his pace, I make a solemn vow to never settle for less.

Unable to hold my orgasm at bay any longer, I clench around him, coming just as fiercely as I did the first time. With his eyes pinned to mine, he continues to pound into me, chasing his own orgasm. I watch in fascination as his face distorts with pleasure and when he groans my name, I swear it is the sweetest sound I have ever heard.

He gives me his weight, burying his face in the crook of my neck and instinctively I wrap my arms and legs around him, holding him to me.

"You're making me soft," I whisper once I've caught my breath.

Lifting his head, he looks down at me.

"Say what?"

"I'm not the girl who has the urge to cuddle after sex."

A blank expression crosses his face before he pushes himself up and starts to roll off me. My legs tighten around his waist, keeping him in place and he raises an eyebrow quizzically.

"But I want to right now," I continue. As soon as the words leave my lips, I feel my cheeks heat. Marco grins back at me and wraps his arms around my waist, rolling us so we're both on our sides, our legs intertwined.

"I like you soft," he says, pressing a quick kiss to my lips. "If it makes you feel better, I don't usually cuddle either."

"Not part of the gentleman code of ethics?"

He laughs, curling a strand of my hair around his finger.

"Actually, you're the first girl to spend the night in my bed."

That surprises me considering he was so adamant about this little sleepover.

"Why me?"

He looks at me thoughtfully before shrugging his shoulders.

"Just feels right."

I guess that's all it takes for someone to let down their guard and change their way of thinking. One feeling, a sense of belonging. It's not something you plan, it just happens. Mostly when you least expect it and sometimes with a person you never imagined being with.

"Now, get some rest. I'm gonna be ready to go again in an hour and this time, I want you on top."

I woke up to the scent of freshly brewed coffee and the sound of bacon sizzling in a frying pan. In other words, I woke to bliss. I had no idea how Marco managed to function so early, especially after sleeping all of three hours. I could barely get it together to take a shower.

But I wasn't complaining.

Last night was single-handedly one of the best nights of my life and this morning wasn't so bad either. After I showered, I joined him in the kitchen for a quick breakfast. He was dressed casually, but his uniform hung on a hook by the door. When it was time for us to get a move on, he grabbed it and draped it over his arm, before pressing his free hand to the small of my back and ushering me out the door. I sort of wished I could've seen him in that uniform again. The first time I was too pissed to truly appreciate it.

Once we were in the car and on the road, I dug into my bag and pulled out my phone. I hadn't bothered to look at it once since he picked me up and it was now dead. Luckily, Marco had a charger in his car, and I plugged it in. As soon as it came on it started dinging with voicemails and text messages. Before I could grab it myself, Marco beat me to it. Lifting it from the center console, he glanced down at the screen briefly before handing it to me.

The screen showed a text alert from my father and one from Hound and a whopping thirteen voicemails. Deciding I would deal with them later, I pulled the phone from the charger and shoved it back in my bag. For the next few minutes we were both silent. I knew Marco had seen Hound's name, and I debated if I should address it, but what would I say? I wasn't ready to break our little bubble and reveal my father was a criminal.

Now, we're a block away from the office and I really don't want to say goodbye. Especially with how much the mood has changed since my phone went off like the Fourth of July.

He pulls into the garage and my stomach plummets when I spot Ritmo parked in his usual spot. The car comes to a halt and I turn just as Marco drops the gear shift into park.

"You're coming up with me?" I ask.

Shit. What if Ritmo tries to talk to me? I don't need a reenactment of the night Marco brought my license to my house.

Flashing me a smile, he opens his door.

"Yeah, I figured we'd tell Soraya the good news."

My eyes must go wide as saucers because he laughs. The last thing I want is to announce to my boss I just spent the night having mind-blowing sex with her friend.

"I don't think that's a good idea," I tell him.

"Why not? Now she can finally get off my back."

"Because it's inappropriate?"

"How is it inappropriate for you and me to have dinner with Tig and Delia? ? It gets them to the party, and that's all Soraya cares about."

My nerves settle slightly.

"Oh, you're talking about next weekend."

He grins at me.

"You thought I was going to march into Soraya's office and tell her I fucked you senseless last night and made you come five times?"

Curling my lip, I smack his arm.

"Very funny."

"She's going to know, Antonia," he says with a laugh. "You're glowing."

"I am not glowing."

"You're smiling. That's just as good as glowing in my book."

Subconsciously I lift a hand to my lips and wouldn't you know it, he's right. I'm smiling and it's not even noon.

"Let's go, before you're late and she thinks it's because we had a quickie in the backseat."

He exits the car and I hurry to do the same, fearing if he rounds the car and opens the door for me, he'll spot Ritmo. I slam the door shut and hurry toward him. Grabbing his hand, I pull him toward the building. Once we hit the doors to the elevator, Marco stabs the button with his thumb and I glance over my shoulder, stealing a glance at Ritmo, who slowly walks toward us. The elevator doors open and Marco steps in. Knowing as soon as he turns around, he'll be face to face with Ritmo, I push Marco against the wall of the elevator and press my lips to his. It's the perfect distraction and by the time the elevator doors close, Marco's got both hands on my ass and I'm fisting his shirt. The elevator dings, and we pull apart.

"What was that for?"

"I'm glowing, remember?" I reply, wiping the lipstick from his lips.

"Yeah, we're a dead giveaway," he mutters as the doors open.

Pulling away from him, I step off the elevator first and find Penelope and Soraya arguing at the reception desk. Their bickering comes to a halt as Marco lets out a whistle and both their gazes shoot to us.

"Good morning, dollface," Marco greets.

Soraya eyes him skeptically.

"Why are you so chipper? Did you arrest a little old lady for jaywalking?"

I laugh and instantly regret it because her eyes dart to me. Crossing her arms over her chest, she raises an eyebrow.

"I guess the edible fruit arrangement worked."

"Like a fucking charm," Marco says, throwing an arm around my shoulders. He pulls me into the crook of his arm and presses a kiss to the top of my head. "Good news, I have it all worked out for next Saturday."

"You figured out how to get them to the party?"

"Yep. After going on and on about Antonia here, Tig told me he wanted to meet her. Antonia has agreed to take one for the team and instead of cutting me loose, she's going to go on another date with me. I'll call him when I get off work and set it up, but I don't see him saying no when it was his idea."

"So, you actually didn't figure out shit."

"Not exactly," he admits. "But it's all taken care of."

Soraya rolls her eyes before looking at me.

"Well, thanks, Antonia. You know, for suffering through another week with this guy," she teases, a smirk playing on her lips.

"No problem," I laugh, feeling embarrassment creep into my cheeks.

"I gotta get out of here," Marco says. "There are bad drivers out there and old lady jaywalkers that I need to save New York City from." If I didn't already want to crawl into a hole and die, you can bet I do the moment he grabs my ass and places a smacking kiss on my lips.

I was so flabbergasted by the kiss, I didn't think what might happen if Marco bumped into Ritmo on his way to work. So for the last hour, I've been debating on whether I should call him or not—you know, just to be sure some crazy biker didn't kidnap him or something.

On top of that, I was prolonging the call to my father.

With any luck, Ritmo didn't kidnap Marco and kill him. Instead, he called my dad and reported that I was safe and sound. I'd still get reamed out when I got back to the compound, but at least the odds of him showing up here with half the club were slim to none.

The sound of Penelope clearing her throat jars my thoughts and I look up at her. In the short time I've known her, I don't think I've seen her smile and judging by the scowl on her face, today's not the day.

"Can I help you with something?" I ask.

"I know what you're doing," she hisses.

I look from her to my computer screen.

I'm pretending to respond to a man who wants advice on how to ask his ex-wife if she'll be his booty call. Unless she has a suggestion, I'm not sure how any of that is her business.

"I see you with that guy every morning and I watch you leave with him every night."

Huh. So she's crazy. Maybe that's why she doesn't smile.

"The guy with all the tattoos," she clarifies. "The gangbanger."

Absorbing her slurs, I try to tame the anger pulsing through me. I may hate what my dad's club stands for, but at the end of the day, the Corrupt Hellraisers are my family. We don't always like our family, but we fucking defend them to small minded people like Penelope.

Fixing her with a glare, I push out of my chair and stand. Instinctively she takes a step back.

Smart girl.

"You don't know shit," I spat.

"I know Marco is a good guy, and he doesn't deserve to be played by the likes of you."

"Not that it's any of your business, but I'm not playing him."

"Then who is the guy?"

"That's none of your business," I grind out, pointing a finger in her face. "I might be the new girl here, but understand this, I don't take kindly to girls getting in my face. Check yourself before you come at me."

"Or what?"

"Do it and you'll find out. Now, if you're done sticking your nose where it doesn't belong, I have work to do. Maybe you can go answer a phone or something."

"Oh please, don't pretend you do anything more than play with Post-its and paperclips. You've yet to meet Ida. Once she gets a load of you, you'll be out the door."

"We'll see about that."

"Stay away from Marco."

"Or what?"

"I'll tell him about your little friend with the teardrop tattoos under his eye."

Like hell, she will.

CHAPTER
SIXTEEN

To say my altercation with Penelope left me in a bad mood would be an understatement of epic proportions. It's obvious the girl is attracted to Marco, but to accuse me of things when she doesn't know my story—that's just wrong and the very reason I have little tolerance for women. It's probably why I don't have a girl tribe or a squad—whatever the trendy name is these days.

The sound of my cell phone ringing jars my thoughts and I peel my eyes away from the emails I'm pretending to work on. Digging into my bag, I pull out my phone and cringe at the sight of my father's contact info. I slide my thumb across the screen and accept the call.

"Hello?"

"You've got five minutes to get your ass down to the garage or I'm coming into your fancy little office and introducing myself to your colleagues."

"Why hello, Dad," I sneer. "Sounds like you're in a great mood."

"I mean it, Antonia. Five fucking minutes."

The line goes dead and I glance at the clock. It's not too early to take my lunch, so I draft Soraya a quick email since she's on a conference call with Ida and I clock out. Realizing I'm going to have to pass Penelope on my way out the door, I shove my AirPods in my ears and crank up the volume, that way if the witch tries to provoke me I won't get locked up on an assault charge.

It works like a charm and I'm in the garage with a minute to spare. Not that it does me any good, it's sixty more seconds of being scolded on how dangerous things are and how reckless I am…yada yada yada.

I spot my father instantly, and of course, he's not alone. His vice president, Cash, stands tall at his right, and next to him is Ritmo and Hound. They all look at me with blank expressions, but as I draw near, I can see the disappointment in Cash's eyes and the disgust in Hound's. Ritmo I can never read. I suppose that's because he looks like a sociopath on any given day. My dad, well, that's another story. He looks like he's about to commit murder.

Great.

"Brought the reinforcements, huh?" I question as I come to a standstill in front of him. "What did I do this time?"

"Who's your fucking boyfriend?" Hound sneers.

"Excuse me?"

"Oh, right, you're just fucking him."

I tear my eyes away from Hound and look to my father, expecting him to put this son of a bitch in his place, but he doesn't move an inch.

"You didn't come home," Cash says. "Didn't check in either."

"I was on a date," I hiss, gritting my teeth. I wave a hand toward my dad. "He knew that."

"You forgot one detail," Dad says.

Is he fucking kidding me?

"Didn't really think you wanted to know I would be spending the night in a guy's bed, but next time I'll call you while we're going at it that way you have peace of mind."

"There ain't going to be a fucking next time, Tonia," Dad hollers.

"Actually, there is, and you don't have a say in that."

"He's a fucking cop!" He shouts so loud it echoes off the walls of the garage. Unfazed by the tone of his voice, I'm taken back by the fact he knows Marco is a cop. I didn't divulge one detail about Marco to my dad. Not his profession. Not his name. Nothing.

"There isn't a chance in Hell you'll be seeing that motherfucker again," Dad continues, his jaw tightening with every word.

I blink for a second before diverting my eyes back to Hound. There was no way he could've known from that night he saw me with Marco that he was a cop.

"How do you know he's a cop?" I ask, looking back at my father.

"That's not important," he seethes, his fists closing and opening as he rolls his neck from side to side. He's not the only one trying to control their anger. My hands are shaking and it's taking every ounce of self-control not to lunge at him.

"You had me followed."

"Of course I had you followed," he fumes. "You gave me no fucking choice. When I say things aren't safe, I'm not blowing smoke, Antonia." He takes a step closer to me. "Ditch the cop or you're going to force my hand."

"What does that even mean?"

"It means we don't need no fucking pig sniffing around our shit," Hound yells.

My gaze slices to him.

"Fuck you," I sneer.

"He's using you, Antonia," Dad growls.

"You're crazy," I murmur in disbelief.

"Maybe, so, but I've been around the block a time or two. He's not interested in you."

That last sentence hits hard.

"Excuse me?" I croak.

"I didn't raise you to be this ignorant," he hisses, roughly combing his fingers through his hair. "The cops are working to bring Bendetti down and that guinea bastard is a rat. He's going to squeal like a pig if he hasn't already and when he does, my name is the first he's gonna give up."

I shake my head. Maybe he's right, maybe I am fucking ignorant because I'm not connecting the dots here.

"What does any of this have to do with me?" I shout.

"He's using you to get to me."

No.

I'm not entertaining this.

No fucking way.

Marco isn't like the rest of them.

Sure, I've had my doubts, but he's proved me wrong every time. Marco wouldn't take advantage of me that way, he wouldn't put on a façade and pretend to be a good guy just to get to my father. A man like that asks questions and forces you to reveal things about yourself. All Marco's done is try to get to know *me*. Not Tank DeLuca's daughter.

I stare at my father. The urge to shake him rolls through me. If only I could make him see the whole world doesn't revolve around him. That I'm a person too and a man can be genuinely attracted to me without having an ulterior motive. That there are good men out there, men who are nothing like the four standing in front of me reading me the riot act.

"He doesn't know I'm your daughter! I haven't said a word about you to him and he hasn't asked."

"Yet," Cash interjects. "It's only a matter of time."

I shake my head as memories from last night begin to assault me. For one night I felt normal. For one night I trusted a man with more than just my body. Am I just supposed to throw that away? Forget how he made me feel? And for what...to ease my father's paranoia? How is that fair?

"End it, Antonia," Dad orders, pulling me away from my head. I lift my chin and meet his gaze. "Before I take the opportunity away and end it for you."

Tank DeLuca doesn't make threats, he only makes promises.

I THOUGHT THE FIRST PART of the day was a nightmare, but after leaving my father and his goons standing in the garage, I realized my morning was a walk in the park. I couldn't get my father's words out of my head and it was affecting my ability to work. Hours later and I still can't stare at the screen without my mind wandering. Luckily, I only have another fifteen minutes on the clock.

Forcing myself to finish my last task, I scroll the submissions. Out of the hundred and sixty that came in today, I narrowed it down to forty-nine. Just as I'm about to send them through to Soraya an idea crosses my mind.

Without giving myself a chance to change my mind, I start typing.

Dear Ida,
The guy I'm seeing isn't anything like anyone I've dated
before. He's respectful, considerate and a God in bed. He's
also a cop. I don't have anything against cops, personally. But
my dad...he's another story. Let's just say my father isn't a
fan. Anyway, I haven't told this new guy my father is a shady
asshole. However, my dad recently found out the guy is a cop
and in not so many words, he told me to dump him. He thinks
the cop is only dating me to put him behind bars or some
crazy shit like that. I really don't think that's the case, but I've
never been a good judge of character. Are all guys assholes?
Is every cop crooked? Or is my father just a paranoid
criminal?
-Anonymous

Pulling my lip between my teeth, I let my eyes scan over the submission. I think it's evasive enough where Soraya won't put two and two together and realize it's me. Before I chicken out, I draw in a deep breath and click send. A quick glance in the lower righthand corner tells me I'm done for the day and I power off my computer.

I grab my stuff and pop my head into Soraya's office. I let her know I sent the submissions through and I say good-bye. Just as I'm about to turn around, a goofy grin spreads across her lips. Suddenly a pair of strong arms wrap around my waist and the familiar scent of Marco's cologne wafts past my nose.

Turning my head, he plants a kiss on my cheek before he spins me around to face him.

"What are you doing here?" I ask, swallowing my shock.

He twirls a strand of my hair around his finger.

"I figured you'd need a ride home since I drove you to work."

I open my mouth to reply, but I notice he's dressed in

his uniform. The navy-blue material clings to all the right places, giving away the fact there's a very hard body beneath those pressed blues of his. A body I wouldn't mind having on top of me again.

For fuck's sake, focus Antonia!

"You're still in your uniform."

"Yeah, and I got the cruiser parked downstairs. If you like I can put the siren on while I drive you home," he offers, wiggling his eyebrows for extra emphasis.

I laugh for two reasons. One, because it sounds completely ridiculous and I can totally see him doing it and two, I can also imagine the horror on my father's face if he saw me pull up in a cop car.

I know it's not funny, but if I don't laugh, I think I might cry, and I don't fucking cry.

"Me and my partner are pulling some overtime and working the 18th Avenue feast tonight. If you don't want to go straight home, you can tag along."

"And what am I supposed to do while you and your partner work?"

"Eat zeppole with me."

Smiling faintly, I shake my head.

Forget Marco, if I don't end things with him, my waistline is going to be in danger, and I can't even blame that on my dad.

"I'm going to gain twenty pounds dating you," I mutter, forgetting all about our audience. I'm sure Penelope is lurking around here too, probably putting the malocchio on me.

"I'm not seeing the issue."

I slap his bicep playfully.

"What do you say, dollface?"

"Actually, I have plans. Can I get a raincheck, though?" I ask hopefully.

I wish I could delete the email I sent through because I don't need advice on what to do.

I'm not ready or willing to give Marco up.

"I'm working for the next couple of nights. What do you say we go Friday night? We can have another sleepover…come to think of it. We can spend the entire weekend together." He pauses and looks over my shoulder at Soraya. "I spoke to Tig and Delia and they're in, so we're all set for the party Saturday night."

"Great," she says. "I'm going to swing by the restaurant on my way home and confirm everything."

He gives her a nod before turning his eyes back to me.

"You sure I can't take you home?"

"Yes, but I'm looking forward to Friday."

He grins.

"Me too, dollface. Me too."

CHAPTER
SEVENTEEN

Marco

AFTER WORKING THE FEAST FOR four nights straight, I had no desire to visit what I once considered my old stomping grounds. The festival of Santa Rosalia or more commonly known as the 18th Ave feast wasn't like I remembered. For starters, it didn't span as many blocks as it used to. The mom and pop shops that sold vintage Italian records and novelties were few and far between and the café's that decorated the corners of every block were on their third and fourth owners. In the years that passed since I was a kid, the feast took on a Hispanic flair, and aside from the traditional Italian foods, there were vendors who sold empanadas and my personal favorite, Mexican street corn.

There were a few things that remained the same. You could still score a slice at DaVinci's Pizzeria and on every block, there was a sausage and pepper stand. You could also find several people selling zeppoles and fried Oreos. If you got there the day the feast opened, you could score some grilled octopus too. There were carnival rides, games, and music blaring from giant speakers. People danced in the street under the festive red, white, and green lights that hung from one streetlight to the next. And the statue of Saint Rosalia was still on display and just as terrifying as it was when I was a kid.

But if you've been to the feast once, you've been a thousand times and when you're working it, breaking up fights and making sure no one steals the dollars pinned to the saint, you'd much rather spend your Friday night curled up on the couch with your girl's legs wrapped around your head.

Antonia, however, has other plans and instead of feasting on her, I'm watching her go to town on a bag of fried Oreos. I'm not complaining. I think one of my favorite things about Antonia is that she isn't shy in front of me. There's nothing worse than being on a date, ordering a steak and a loaded baked potato, and having the woman you're with pretend she's satisfied with the arugula on her plate. You know the second you drop her at her door, she's fixing herself a sandwich.

Not Antonia, though.

If only I could get her to be as open and honest about the rest of her life as she is with her appetite, I might consider her my dream girl. She still hasn't told me who her father is and won't let me anywhere near her house. I tried to drive her home on Monday, and she brushed me off. After that, she got real quiet on me. Every time I called or text, she'd rush me off the phone or give me one-word answers. I couldn't be mad, though, because I had given her the same treatment the week before.

Then Thursday rolled around, and she was chipper as fuck. She flirted with me and sent me pics of herself in about a half a dozen outfits, asking me which I liked best for Tig and Delia's party. Truth be told, she looked fantastic in everything, but we decided on a black leather mini skirt and a red crop top. I couldn't fucking wait until tomorrow, especially since I convinced her that underwear was not an option with that skirt.

Anyway, I think she might be bipolar.

It's okay, I dig it.

What I don't dig is that fuck who follows her around. According to the database, his road name is Ritmo. I noticed he was lurking around the parking garage when I dropped her off on Tuesday morning and that's why I hijacked Richie and our cruiser to swing by her office and offer her a ride home, which of course, she declined.

I don't think he is out to harm her, though. From what I gather about these guys, they pride themselves on some sort of brotherhood and when they're not fucking the law, they take care of one another's family. I want to believe this Ritmo character is following Antonia for protection, but that worries me too because I have no idea what she needs protection from. A guy like Tank Deluca has a lot of enemies and any street guy knows the way to hurt a man is to go after what he loves.

"You know I'm disappointed in you," Antonia says.

The sound of her voice forces me back to the present. My brows draw together as I study her for a moment. She lifts a fried Oreo to my lips and grins. "I thought you would eat me under the table."

I raise an eyebrow.

Now, we're talking.

"Find a table and it's on."

She laughs and gives my chest a playful punch.

"I don't mean that. Take a bite," she encourages, pressing the artery clogging dessert to my lips. Sticking out my tongue, I get a taste of the powdered sugar before she pushes the entire Oreo into my mouth. Chewing, I watch as a satisfied smirk crosses her lips. Unable to help myself, I dip my head and crash my lips against hers. She licks the excess sugar from my lips before pushing her tongue into my mouth. My hands slide around her waist, and I pull her closer. In a crowded street, she's all that exists, and that's just as terrifying as the chipped saint wearing the black frizzy wig.

She breaks the kiss first and reaches up to finger the gold horn dangling from my neck.

"I think I need one of these," she says.

"An Italian horn?"

"It wards off the malocchio."

"It's supposed to," I say.

"I'm pretty sure Penelope wants me dead after your little display of affection on Tuesday. Is there a place I can get one here?"

Lacing our fingers together, I laugh.

"There's a shop one block up that sells them. We can get you a horn and a shirt that says, *"Italians Do It Better."* You can wear it to bed after I fuck you senseless."

"I thought you prefer me naked."

"I do, but my apartment can be drafty."

She loops her arm through mine and I lead her to the little shop on the corner of 69th Street. We grab a horn and two shirts. Just as I'm about to check out, Antonia stops me and asks the little old man helping us if he has anything to honor Saint Gerard that we could purchase.

It's not necessarily an odd request, my mom prays to Saint Anthony every morning. I guess I wasn't expecting Antonia to be much of a holy roller.

"Is that your patron saint?"

She shakes her head.

"Saint Gerard is the patron saint of fertility. I thought maybe we could get something for Tig and Delia." She pauses, pulling her lower lip between her teeth as she lifts her gaze to me. "Wait, is that insensitive? How would you feel if you're meeting someone for the first time and she hands you a prayer card to help with your infertility?" She shakes her head. "Oh, God, forget it. You said the whole point of the party was to get their mind off their struggles and here I am suggesting we throw it in their faces. Forget it, sir!"

I touch a hand to her cheek and coax her eyes back to mine.

"I think it's very thoughtful."

"Really?"

I nod just as the man returns holding a silver bracelet. It has a charm of St. Gerard, and on the back, there is a prayer.

"Let's get it," I say.

"Okay, but maybe we'll give it to them after the party or even another day," she suggests, and I agree. I pay the man for our stuff and Antonia takes the bag. As we exit the shop, she spots the Saint Rosalia statue across the street.

"What is that?"

"That's Saint Rosalia."

"Why does the saint have a wig on?"

"I've been asking myself the same question since I'm six years old."

According to my mother's logic, the saint is old and chipped, and the organizers of the feast try to preserve her by dressing her up like a streetwalker, hence the black wig and dress, which is a new addition this year.

"You know, I always wondered why people pin dollars to the saint," she says. "I even googled it after I went to the San Gennaro festival in Little Italy, but I couldn't really find an answer. Some people say it's sacrilegious, but if you think about it, it's really not all that different than lighting a candle in church. Most of the time the candles are in front of saints."

She's got a point.

"I never really thought of it like that," I say, eyeing the statue. "Should we pin a dollar?"

"Why not?"

She grabs my hand and drags me across the street. Digging into my pocket, I pull out a couple of singles and hand them to Antonia. She rolls them and grabs a pin from the statue, threading the tip through the dollar. Once it's fixed to the saint's dress, she rolls another dollar and hands it to me. It's the first time I'm partaking in the tradition and I make the sign of the cross when I'm done, just as I would if I was lighting a candle.

Turning back to Antonia, I grab her hand and pull her against me. I press my lips to hers and she winds her arm winds around my neck. Angling her head, she gives me better access and my tongue slides past her lips. I devour her shamelessly on the street, in front of the saint.

"My dick was in that mouth."

The blood in my veins instantly turns to ice as I pull away from Antonia and turn around. Standing five feet away is Hound. I don't hesitate for a second. I charge at him, grabbing him by his kutte. He tries to shrug me off, but I spin him around and pummel him into the grotto holding the beloved saint. Someone screams and before I realize what I'm doing, my fist rears back and collides with Hound's face. Not once. Not even twice. I do it over and over until my knuckles are bloody and I hear Antonia beg me to stop.

The next thing I know, someone is pulling me off Hound. I turn around and I'm surrounded by five or six men, all of them wearing the same insignia as the man I just beat the shit out of. Antonia pushes her way past them and stands with her back to me.

"Don't you dare," she shouts.

"Get out of the way, Tonia," one of them demands. I narrow my eyes as the man steps forward and sure as shit, it's Tank DeLuca.

Great.

CHAPTER
EIGHTEEN

ANTONIA

M Y BODY SHAKES WITH ANGER as I keep my eyes pinned to my dad's. Swallowing, I force myself to find my voice.

"If you have any love for me whatsoever you will stop this right now or I swear, you'll never see me again. I am done. Do you hear me? Done!"

"This has nothing to do with you," he argues.

My eyes bulge in disbelief.

"Are you kidding me? Hound just disgraced me in front of all these people. It has everything to do with me."

Crossing his arms against his chest, my father spits the toothpick hanging from his lips into the street and looks from me to Marco who is standing directly behind me.

"It looks to me like a cop just assaulted an innocent bystander at a festival and in turn destroyed public property."

Before Marco or I can respond, Cash walks up to my father.

"His nose is broken, boss. We gotta get Doc on the horn," he tells him.

"He's lucky that's all that's broke," Marco snarls.

I tear my gaze away from my father as Marco moves to stand next to me. Rubbing his bloody knuckles on the front of his tee, he pierces me with a look. As angry as he is, there is nothing but concern flashing in his eyes. "You okay?"

"I'm fine."

He assesses me for a moment before turning his attention to my dad.

"Marco…" I murmur.

Ignoring me, he shakes out his swollen fist and steps toward my dad.

"You her father?"

"You going to pretend like you don't know who I am?"

"I know if I had a daughter, and a man disrespected her the way your pal just did, I'd be shaking the hand of the man who rearranged his face and getting a few punches in myself."

Dad laughs.

"That so?"

"Yeah, it is," Marco says, confidently. "You want to call 9-1-1 and tell them I assaulted that piece of shit, go ahead. Tell dispatch I say hello. But do it before you lose your shot because in five minutes, I'm taking your daughter out of here and I'm going to spend the rest of the night erasing that fool from her mind."

"You hear him, Cash? This guy is trying to tell me how to handle my daughter."

"With all due respect, sir, your daughter is a grown woman and in case you haven't noticed, she can handle herself just fine. However, she doesn't have to handle shit because so long as she's with me I'll happily take the trash out where she's concerned."

Oh, wow.

It's probably not a good time to ask Marco if he wants to get married and have babies, right?

No man has ever defended my honor or stood up to my father before.

Instead of proposing, I move to his side and loop my arm through his. He turns his head slightly and gives me a wink.

Yeah, I'm totally marrying this one.

"You're fucking dead," Hound hisses.

We both turn at the sound of his voice and find Mouse and Ritmo holding him up. His face is a mess, and there is blood dripping from his chin.

"You hear me, motherfucker, I said you're dead."

"Careful," Dad warns.

"Fuck that! He broke my nose."

"It was an ugly nose anyway," I point out.

Deciding he's not worth my time, I look back at Marco.

"You ready to get out of here?" he questions.

I give him a quick nod before looking back at my dad. His expression is blank and to my surprise, he doesn't say a word. The silent treatment is new for us and I don't know what to make of it. If I'm being honest, I'm not even sure I care. I'm more concerned with what Marco is thinking and feeling.

I shrug my bag high on my shoulder and give Marco's arm a squeeze. He takes my cue and starts to lead me away. As we're about to pass my father, he leans forward.

"You're making a mistake, Antonia."

Those words make me freeze. How can he still think

Marco is anything but sincere when he just attacked Hound on my behalf? If there was any doubt in my mind that Marco's intentions weren't pure, they are obliterated.

"If I'm making a mistake, it's mine to make. Surely, you can understand that seeing as you have made so many yourself." I turn my head. "Let's go, please."

Marco nods, and without another word, we walk away from them. We make our way through the crowd and are stopped by two police officers. They question Marco, but he doesn't give away much. All he tells them is there was a disagreement before pulling me away.

In the car, he remains silent and I try to decide how I'm going to come clean about everything. Now that he's met my father there is no use in hiding any part of my life from him. If this is going to go anywhere, he should be aware of how thoroughly fucked up my family is.

I steal a glance at him from the corner of my eye.

"How's your hand?"

He flexes it around the steering wheel and cringes, but he doesn't say anything. Another minute passes before he slows for a light and draws out a deep breath.

"Is your father always such a dick?" he questions. He must regret the words because he closes his eyes and shakes his head. "I'm sorry, I—"

"No," I interrupt, pausing to pinpoint exactly when my father went from being my best friend to my number one enemy. "He started to lose his shit when I took the job at "Ask Ida" and then when he found out I was dating a cop that just drove him over the edge."

"He doesn't like cops, huh?"

I cock my head to the side and study him.

"C'mon Marco," I murmur softly. "You saw his vest. You probably know better than I do what kind of man my dad is. He doesn't play well with your kind."

His fingers tighten around the steering wheel.

"What exactly is my kind? Because I didn't see your dad putting that asshole in his place."

"That's not what I meant." Sighing, I push the hair away from my eyes and turn my attention toward the window. "He doesn't trust cops, okay? He thinks they're all out to get him and the only reason you're dating me is because you want to get close to him."

The minute he slams his foot on the brake, I feel his eyes on me.

"What did you just say?" he asks.

A horn honks behind us, causing me to sneak a glance at the sideview mirror.

"Marco, you're holding up traffic."

"I don't give a fuck," he grinds out. "Look at me, Antonia."

Hesitantly, I turn my head and drag my eyes to his.

"Two weeks ago, I was sitting outside the Brooklyn Battery Tunnel in my cruiser when a motorcycle zoomed past me and blew through a red light. I flipped my siren on and pulled you over. I didn't know jack shit about you other than you were the most gorgeous thing I ever laid eyes on. Then I got a dose of your smart mouth, and I was hooked. It was pure chance that you wound up working for Soraya, and I spent most of our lunch asking about you. I brought you your license because I needed to see you again. I thought if I got you out of my system, I could forget our paths ever crossed, but I was only fooling myself. You're not the kind of girl you purge or even forget and I'm starting to think we would've found one another whether you worked for "Ask Ida" or not."

"Traffic court," I whisper.

He reaches across the console and touches his good hand to my cheek.

"I don't give a fuck about your father or what he does. It's not the reason I wake up anxious to see your face or hear your voice."

I swallow hard, emotion clogging my throat. A whole slew of horns beep behind us and one driver shouts for us to "move our fucking car"—we ignore both.

"I didn't want to believe him."

"Then don't because he's full of shit," he grinds out, dropping his hand away from my cheek. He turns his head and brings both hands to the steering wheel, gripping it as tight as his battered knuckles allow.

"You and Hound…" He bites the side of his cheek and his jaw goes rigid. "You said he wasn't your boyfriend."

"He wasn't."

"But you were involved."

"Briefly," I admit. "That's over, Marco."

He gives that some thought. His eyes slice back to mine, and he shakes his head.

"It's not for him," he says in a gravel tone.

If I had it in me, I might've laughed. It was over for Hound before it even started, but I doubt Marco wants to hear any of that. He draws out a deep breath and rolls down his window. Turning his head, he shouts for the offensive horn blowers to fuck off and slams his foot on the gas.

We ride to his apartment in silence. Once we make our way inside, I go straight into the kitchen and open his freezer. Popping some ice cubes from the tray, I wrap them in a dishtowel and make my way into the living room.

"I got you…" my words fade as he pulls his shirt over his head. "Ice…I got you some ice for your hand."

"Thanks, but I think I'm going to take a shower," he says, closing the distance between us. "Make yourself at home," he adds before giving my lips a quick peck.

Something feels off with him, but we've both had quite the night. Emotions are high, and I suppose I've given him a lot to absorb. Nothing will throw a guy into a tailspin like revealing your dad is a notorious biker with a rap sheet.

"Right," I say, lifting the dishtowel awkwardly. "I'll just go put this in the freezer in case you change your mind after the shower."

He gives me another peck and disappears down the hallway. I go to the kitchen and put the towel with the ice back in the freezer. A moment later I hear the shower running in the bathroom and I make my way back into the living room. Taking a seat on the couch, I drop my head into my hands and my father's face flashes before me. I wonder if he heard what Hound said or if he walked up afterward. I like to think he wouldn't let his protégé talk about me like that, but the man I saw tonight was a different version of the man who raised me. Tonight, I was treated to the side of him he preserves for his rivals and I didn't like it. I don't know what happens now.

Even if by some miracle I can smooth things over with my dad, I don't want to be anywhere near Hound.

His words replay in my head, and I cringe.

I can't believe I got involved with him. That I gave him the ammunition he used against me tonight. I guess that is what happens when a girl has horrible self-esteem. She kneels for some undeserving prick, hoping she'll hold his interest a little longer. It doesn't work, and he throws her aside like she's yesterday's trash. She wonders what she could've done to keep him. What she did wrong. But it's not her. It's him and that's something she doesn't realize until another man comes along and kneels for *her*.

Suddenly I'm on my feet, pulling my shoes and clothes off as I pad down the hallway. Reaching the bathroom, I turn the knob and push the door open. Steam immediately engulfs me as I step inside. I spot Marco through the foggy shower glass. Keeping his head bowed and his good hand braced against the tiles, he lets the water stream down his back.

I swallow at the sight of him as my feet carry me closer. His head lifts and he turns, his eyes find mine through the glass before trailing the length of my bare body. Silently, he opens the shower door and I step inside.

His gaze continues to rake over me, pausing at my chest and I notice his cock jutting between us, fully erect. My fingers itch to touch, my mouth begs for a taste.

I lick my lips and take a step closer.

"Is this okay?"

He doesn't reply with words, instead, he backs me up against the cool tiles and lowers his mouth to mine. A moan rumbles deep in my throat as his tongue slides along mine. Reaching between us, my fingers close around his thick cock. Using slow, even strokes, I work his shaft, letting my thumb occasionally caress the head.

He groans into my mouth before breaking the kiss and touching his forehead to mine. With his eyes cast downward, he watches as I cup his balls with my other hand.

"Christ," he hisses.

"You like that?" I whisper.

"I fucking love it," he rasps, meeting my gaze.

"Then maybe you'll love this too," I say. Keeping my eyes on his, I drop to my knees.

"What are you doing…no."

"No?"

"Antonia, you don't have to—"

"I don't have to do anything," I say, cutting him off. "I want to."

As I say the words, I realize I wholeheartedly mean

them. I want him this way. I want to watch him fall apart at the mercy of my mouth and not because I'm desperate to keep him, but rather because I want to feel that intimacy with him and only him.

He pushes his fingers through my hair and his hand molds to the back of my head as my lips part and my tongue touches the tip of his cock, slowly circling it. Inhaling a sharp breath, his nostrils flare. I lick the underside of his shaft and angle my head. My tongue flicks his balls before my lips slowly trail up his veiny cock. Opening my mouth wider, I take him in. Inch by inch until the head of his cock touches the back of my throat and I gag on it. As a knee jerk reaction, my eyes begin to water but I don't tear them away from his.

Closing my lips tightly around him, I start to suck. My head bobs up and down as my fingers curl around the backs of his thighs.

My eyes plead with him to move.

To take.

To fuck.

His control finally snaps and he fists my hair. Jerking his hips, he thrusts deeper and deeper. My fingers dig into his thighs as I open wider. Drops of pre-cum slide down my throat and he quickly pulls out of my mouth.

"It's okay," I croak, reaching for him.

He shakes his head and untangles his fingers from my hair. Pulling me to my feet, he spins me around and plasters me against the wall. I gasp the second my sensitive nipples touch the tile and spread my legs. Pressing his cock against my ass, he gathers my soaking wet hair and wraps it around his bruised fist. Biting through the pain, he pulls my hair and turns my head. His lips crash against mine and his tongue wastes no time entering my mouth.

The ache between my legs intensifies and I break the kiss.

"Please," I beg as his mouth drops to my neck. He sucks and nibbles, making his way to my shoulder.

"Say it," he growls, pressing his dick against my ass harder. "Tell me your mine. Tell me I'm the only one who fucks you from now on."

"I'm yours," I pant. "Please...I..." my words fade into a moan as he reaches between my legs and touches my clit. "Just you." My eyes roll as he circles my clit. "You're the only one I want fucking me," I cry.

His fingers leave me, and his knee moves between my legs, spreading them further apart. I brace my palms against the wall of the shower and prepare myself. With one hand on my hip and the other still pulling my hair, he thrusts deep inside me, feeding me every inch. My knees buckle against the tile and I moan his name.

"Fuck," he growls.

In an instant he finds a rhythm, pulling out and plunging in. My pussy stretches and my legs wobble as I try to keep up, but it doesn't take long for my orgasm to cripple me. Moaning his name, I close my eyes and surrender to the pleasure coursing through my body.

Marco continues to pump in and out of me. He untangles my hair from his fingers and moves his hand to my other hip, holding me steady as he rotates his hips and fucks me.

Harder.

Deeper.

One orgasm rolls into two and then another.

I can barely stand when I feel him pull out of me, but I force myself to turn around. With my back pressed against the wall, I watch him jerk his cock. His release spurts out, decorating his hand.

"Look at me," I whisper breathlessly.

His eyes snap to mine as he continues to pull his release from his body.

"You're mine too."

CHAPTER
NINETEEN

Marco

I COULD GET USED TO waking up to Antonia's hair draped across my chest and her soft body curled against my side. A shocking thought for a man who swore he'd never engage in sleepovers of any kind. I had long ago mastered the art of goodbyes and creeping out of a woman's bed before she woke and yet, here I am, perfectly content watching her sleep.

There's no fear of getting too attached when it comes to Antonia.

I knew things were different with her before last night, but after the showdown with Hound and meeting her old man, something shifted between us. She left the feast with me, taking a stand against her father. She even divulged the details of her relationship with Hound and Tank's crazy suspicion that I was using her to get to him. Her trust and honesty spoke volumes, but it wasn't until we were back at my apartment and in my shower that I realized how deep things were getting. It didn't matter where she came from or who she was with; I wanted her to be mine, and in the shower, that's exactly what she became.

Mine.

I don't know what happens from here, but so long as she's game, we can take it one step at a time and see where it goes. With any luck, we will go the distance and I can spend every morning just like this.

Winding the ends of her hair around my finger, I kiss the top of her head. She stirs slightly, hooking her leg over mine as she nestles closer to me.

Yeah, I can definitely get used to this.

"What time is it?" she groans.

With my free hand, I reach for my phone. My hand is still fucked up from the beating I threw Hound, but I'll live. Unfortunately, so will he. I glance at the time on the screen before tossing the thing back on the nightstand.

"A little after ten," I say, wrapping both arms around her. Sliding them down her back, I reach the hem of the t-shirt she's wearing—an old NYPD shirt I got when I played in a charity softball game. Finding her bare ass, I grab both cheeks and pull her on top of me. Why she bothered with a t-shirt at all when she opted for no panties remains a mystery. I prefer her naked on all counts…and while we're at it, on all fours.

Her head juts from my chest, and she stares at me with groggy eyes. Lifting the shirt, I drag it up her body, over her perky tits. Unable to help myself, I lean forward and take one perfectly pert nipple into my mouth. After a moment, I release it with a smack of my lips and pull the shirt over her head. Her mass of curls hangs wildly, framing her face. The ends kiss the tops of her breasts and the vision of her is like a punch to the gut.

There's nothing more perfect.

Nothing more beautiful.

I lift my gaze back to hers.

"That's better," I say huskily, bringing her back to my chest. I kiss the top of her head and let my hands travel over the globes of her ass, to her back, pressing her closer.

"You're dangerous, Pirelli."

"No more than you, DeLuca," I murmur.

She lifts her head from my chest, and our eyes meet. Touching a hand to her cheek, I wet my lips.

"You hungry?" I ask. "We can DoorDash breakfast."

Cocking her head to the side, she eyes me curiously, a small smile playing on her full lips.

"What happened to the master chef who cooked me breakfast last week?"

"He'd much rather feast on you. If we order now, that gives us about twenty minutes or so before the dasher knocks on the door."

"Hmm…" she murmurs.

Pushing up on my chest until she's fully seated on top of me, she runs her hands up my body. My eyes drop between her legs and I growl at the sight of her bare pussy—already wet and begging for attention. It's nice to know we're on the same page, seeing as my dick has been ready for over an hour.

"Or we can just eat later. The party isn't until eight, right?" she asks, lifting her hands to her tits. She rolls her nipples between her fingers, and I lose all train of thought.

"What was the question?"

"The party…it's not until later, right?"

"Yeah, we got all day," I croak as she releases her nipples. I reach out to tease them with my own fingers when she suddenly rolls off me.

"Shit!"

"What the hell just happened?" I ask, staring at my fully erect cock.

In an instant, she's out of the bed, pacing in all her naked glory.

"My clothes."

Why the fuck her clothes are a concern right now boggles my mind, but I play along.

"They are here somewhere but I assure you they're not needed at the moment," I say, looking back at my cock. The poor thing looks like it's going to explode. My eyes slice back to Antonia. "Can you come back here?"

We need you.

Stat.

"The outfit for the party," she clarifies. "The skirt and the shirt, my boots…it's at the clubhouse." Bringing her hands to her head, she threads her fingers roughly through her curls. "I'm such an idiot," she berates before resuming the pacing.

I'm fucking dizzy just watching her, or maybe that's not the case at all. Perhaps I'm feeling lightheaded because all my blood is in my groin.

"I was trying to hide the fact I was a byproduct of a criminal from you, I had no intention of getting dressed there or having you pick me up from there so why the hell didn't I pack my shit?" She freezes mid rant, and it becomes clear my dick isn't getting any relief anytime soon.

"Oh God."

What did she forget now? Her comb? Perhaps her birth control.

That last one sobers me up.

I didn't wear a condom in the shower, something I realized last night, but between then and now I had done a marvelous job of pushing it out of my head.

Sitting up, I lean my back against the headboard and

call her name. She snaps out of her meltdown for a second and looks at me.

"Everything I own is at the clubhouse," she reveals. "Including my bike."

I was expecting we'd need to have this conversation, I just figured we'd be having it Monday morning when the bubble burst and everyday life resumed.

"Were you not planning on going back?"

As the question leaves my lips, I think about what that would mean. I'm certainly not opposed to the idea, but I'm also very aware of how crazy that sounds. She can't hide here forever. I may have my opinions about Tank DeLuca, but that's all they are.

Opinions.

He is her dad and like him or not, he's part of her life.

"No…yes…I don't know," she sighs frustratedly.

Sighing, I throw my legs over the edge of the bed and grab a pair of sweats from the floor. If we are going to have this conversation, it's best one of us has some fucking clothes on. Pulling the pants up my legs, the elastic band slaps against my abs and I turn to face her.

"You're freaking out for no reason."

Her eyes bulge and I amend my sentence.

"Okay, you're freaking out with good reason, but let's take a step back and calm down, okay? I'll take you over there to get what you need."

"You really think that's a good idea? You broke Hound's nose. We won't make it past the gates."

That angered me.

Sure, I broke the bastard's nose, but he deserved it and if Tank heard him say what he said, I think the guy would agree. That's of course, if he was a levelheaded man who didn't go to jail for assaulting cops.

She's right.

We're fucked.

I'm not about to tell that to Antonia, though.

"Look, your father has a problem with me. He's cooked up this crazy theory in his head that I'm the enemy without knowing a damn thing about me other than my profession. I don't like what he does, but he's your father and instead of writing him off, I'll give him the courtesy of getting to know me and see my intentions are pure, that I'm more than a badge and a pair of handcuffs."

Her face softens, and the panic flees her features.

"If you think it's better, I'll stay in the car, outside the gates, fine. You just call me if you need me. And if you decide you want to hold off on going there today, we can go to the mall and get you something to wear tonight. Tomorrow, you won't need any clothes."

"Oh, yeah? Why is that?"

"You'll be naked all day."

"So much for pure intentions," she laughs.

"I should've been more specific."

"Surprise!"

Tig and Delia freeze in their tracks, their eyes moving from me to take in the rest of the room and all the familiar faces of their friends.

"What's all this?" Tig asks, looking back at me.

Grinning at the bastard, I shrug my shoulders and raise my beer to him.

"Happy Anniversary," Soraya says, rushing toward them. Graham is hot on her heels as she envelopes Delia in a hug.

"They look genuinely surprised," Antonia says from beside me. Taking a pull of my beer, I turn to her. She decided to hold off on paying her father a visit to get some of her things and after a morning quickie, we hit Kings Plaza. I was never big on shopping, but that might be because I never got to sit in a dressing room while my girl slid into one sexy outfit after another. It's a totally different experience.

Out of all the clothes she bought, she decided to wear a simple off the shoulder black dress that molded to every curve. It was cut mid-thigh, and she paired it with knee-high boots. Another new purchase I was sure was only made to drive me mad. I couldn't wait to get her home. She could ditch the dress, but the boots were staying on.

Peeling her gaze away from Tig and Delia, she looks at me as I lower the bottle from my lips and stare at hers.

The red lipstick is new too.

I can't wait to smear it.

"Aren't we going to go say hello?"

"We should probably do that, right?"

She laughs and grabs my free hand.

"Introduce me to your cousins, Pirelli. Isn't that why you brought me here?"

A week ago, bringing Antonia here to meet Tig seemed like the perfect excuse to get him and Delia here, but now I just want her here for me. Before I can tell her that, though, she drags me to the small huddle surrounding our guests of honor.

Graham notices me first.

"Pirelli, nice to see you finally decided to ease up on the hair gel," he mocks. "How's your jaw?"

"Bennett," I reply. "Still got that stick shoved up your ass, huh? Must be painful when you take a shit."

He chuckles and offers me his hand, which I take.

"Antonia, you've met Graham, right?"

"Yes," she replies, flashing him a brilliant smile. "Nice to see you again."

"Likewise, I hear all good things from Soraya," he replies, eyeing her empty glass. "What are you drinking?"

She follows his gaze.

"Tequila on the rocks."

"Looks like you can use a refill," Graham says, reaching for her glass. He lifts his eyes to me. "You need another?"

"I'm good, thanks."

He nods, and then Tig's boisterous voice cuts through all the background noise.

"Is this the girl you keep gushing about? Delia, babe, get over here. She's real!"

Antonia giggles as I refrain from elbowing him in the gut. Instead, I drape an arm around Antonia's shoulders, bringing her closer. I should've gone for her waist, her silky skin under my fingertips is too tempting.

"Tig, Delia, this is Antonia. Antonia, this asshole is my cousin and the beauty on his arm is up for sainthood for marrying him."

"Nice to meet you both. Happy Anniversary," she says, offering her hand to Tig.

He looks at it and then laughs before pulling her out of my arms and into his.

"We hug around here."

"I like hugs," Antonia replies.

The three of them exchange pleasantries and a few laughs at my expense.

"You're smiling so hard right now," Soraya says as she snatches my beer from my hands and downs it herself. I peel my eyes away from Tig, Antonia, and Delia and look at her.

"Your husband is on a drink run, should we flag him down?"

She hands me back the empty bottle.

"I like her, Marco."

"Look at that, another thing we have in common."

She flits her gaze to me.

"I don't mean as an intern," she clarifies. "I like her for you. Don't fuck it up."

"I don't plan to," I reply instantly, my eyes darting back to Antonia. I watch as she throws her head back and laughs at something Tig says. His eyes twinkle as he grins at her, a sure sign that she's won him over too.

"We did good," Soraya says. "They look happy."

Delia joins Antonia and the two of them smack Tig playfully.

"Yeah, they do," I agree.

It was definitely worth all the craziness to see them smile again, even if it's only for one night. Graham returns just as the tempo of the music changes and a classic free-style song starts to play.

"I love this song," Soraya says, taking the drinks from Graham. She hands them to me and grabs him by the tie, dragging him onto the dance floor. Shaking my head at the crazy lovebirds, I make my way to Antonia.

"I pierced my tongue once," Antonia says, and I nearly drop the drinks.

"What?" I croak.

Why couldn't I have pulled her over during that stage in her life?

"I hated it," she continues. "My tongue swelled, and I couldn't talk. I wound up pulling it out."

"I pierced Soraya's tongue," Delia tells her.

"Do you do tattoos too?"

"Nah, that's all me," Tig says, raising his beer. He points the neck of it towards her. "You got ink?"

"Not yet."

Christ.

"I have something in mind, though," she continues.

"Oh, yeah?" I ask, totally intrigued.

Her eyes sparkle with mischief as they meet mine.

"Yep."

"You going to share?"

She shakes her head and looks back at Tig.

"Can you fit me in this week?"

"I always have time for a blank canvas. How's Tuesday?"

"I get out of work at five."

"You're in."

"Wait a minute," I say. "You still haven't finished the piece on my back."

"You did that?" Antonia questions. She finally takes the drink from my hand, but she doesn't make eye contact with me. She's too enthralled with Tig. If Delia wasn't standing right there, and he didn't have his hand on his wife's ass, I might be jealous.

"Guilty."

"I love it," she says and my eyes snap back to her. I hadn't even realized she noticed the damn thing. She must sense I'm staring because she finally turns to me. "I was admiring it this morning when you were in the shower."

A guest of the party shouts for Tig and Delia to join him at the bar for shots and they excuse themselves, leaving us alone.

"I love them," she says, once they're out of earshot. I know I should probably ease her worries of being accepted by my family and tell her it's obvious the feeling is mutual, but I'm stuck on the tattoo thing.

"Tell me more about this tattoo."

"Nope, you'll just have to stick around and see for yourself."

It's not even up for debate.

There is no place I would rather be.

No one else I would rather be with.

A fact that is only confirmed as the night goes on and Antonia is welcomed into the bunch. She tears up the dance floor with Soraya, does shots with Tig and Delia, and even pokes fun at Graham's suit and she does it all with a smile on her face.

A smile that knocks me on my ass.

I've been the guy on the outside looking in, watching everyone find love and I never thought I was missing anything.

Until tonight.

Until Antonia.

We may be from two different worlds, but she fits in mine.

I just need to figure out how the hell I'm going to convince her I fit into hers.

CHAPTER TWENTY

Marco

THE SOUND OF THE SMOKE alarm wakes me, and I spring out of bed. I drag my naked ass into the kitchen where I find Antonia. My t-shirt barely covers her ass as she stands on her tiptoes, waving a dishtowel at the smoke alarm. Coming up behind her, I grab the towel with one hand and unscrew the alarm from the ceiling. The annoying beeping sound stops instantly.

"Thank God," she exclaims, pushing her hair out of her face. "That thing was driving me insane."

"What happened?" I ask, looking toward the stove and the charred frying pan. "Are those black things pancakes?"

"They're a little well done."

"I'll say," I mutter, tearing my eyes away from her attempt at breakfast.

She frowns.

"I can't cook."

"Noted," I reply, trying not to laugh because she looks

like she might burst into tears. Tossing the dishtowel on the counter, I wrap my arms around her waist and pull her close. I bend my head and press my lips to hers. "Good morning."

"It was until I ruined breakfast."

"I'm naked in case you haven't noticed, it's still a great morning," I tease, dipping my head to kiss her neck. You would think after the last few sleepovers she'd realize I'm content with having her for breakfast. I could probably sustain with having her for lunch and dinner too.

Lifting her in my arms, she winds her legs around my hips, and I carry her to the couch. I gently deposit her against the cool leather and drop to my knees. Spreading her legs, my hands travel up the inside of her thighs as I eye her sleek pussy.

She is always shamelessly wet and waiting for me.

"What about breakfast?"

"I'm about to have mine. We'll get you something to nosh on later."

A giggle spills from the back of her throat as I lift her legs onto my shoulders. I settle between her thighs and press my mouth to her sweet center. My tongue takes one languid stroke and flicks her clit.

"You spoil me," she moans, threading her fingers through my hair.

After last night, I'm going to have to disagree. I'm the spoiled one, I was the envy of every man at the party. On top of winning over Tig and Delia and scoring us an invitation for dinner at their house next weekend, she rocked my world when we got home. If fucking was a sport, we were Olympians.

"Marco…" she cries, clawing my back.

I'm just getting started, and she's already about to come. Like I said, gold medal champ over here.

"Marco the door!"

My mouth pauses and I lift my eyes to hers.

"What?"

"Someone's at your door," she pants.

Another knock sounds, but I don't move from my position between her legs. In fact, I'm about to go down on her again and ignore whoever it is intruding at this ungodly hour when I hear my mother's shrill voice.

"Marco Vincenzo Pirelli I know you're in there!"

Kicking me away, Antonia sits up.

"Who is that?"

"Satan."

Leaning back on my haunches, I roughly comb my fingers through my hair. The pounding on the door continues and I mutter a curse before turning back to Antonia. Anger flashes in her eyes and she gives me another nudge with her foot.

"A woman is banging on your door at eight o'clock on a Sunday while your head is between my legs. Care to explain?"

"Sure," I say, rising to my feet. "Why don't you go put on a pair of panties, so my mother doesn't see how wet your pussy is when I open the door. Oh, and while you're at it, do you mind grabbing me a pair of shorts? It's been a while since my mother has seen my 'peeschadiel' as she likes to call it."

Her eyes nearly bulge out of their sockets.

"Your mother is here!?" she shrieks, jumping to her feet.

"Marco, I know you're in there! Don't make me call the super."

"Oh my God," Antonia hisses. "Look at me."

"Still naked over here," I say, waving a hand down the length of me. "At least you got a shirt. Smart move. I get it now."

"I can't meet your mother."

"Well, you can and you're about to…so again, panties. Now." I turn back to the door. "Coming!"

Or at least Antonia would've been if you hadn't decided to show up.

I would have been next.

By some miracle of God, Antonia springs into action and scampers into my bedroom. A pair of basketball shorts come flying out of the room and I hurry to grab them. Shoving my legs through them, I make a dash for the door.

If only I paid attention during the religious instruction classes, she made me take for six years, I might be able to send a prayer up to the man upstairs. But instead of learning the Hail Mary, I was making googly eyes at the sixteen-year-old student teaching the class.

Maybe this is my penance for that.

Pulling open the door, I swipe my hand over my mouth.

You know that saying, *'do you kiss your mother with that mouth?'*

We're about to find out.

"Mom, what a surprise!"

"Oh, cut the crap," she says, smacking me in the head with her purse—a Louis Vuitton knock off she scored on Canal Street. Luckily, she completed the transaction before me, and Richie raided the place. Imagine having to arrest your mother for buying a fake handbag in the back room of a fruit market. Actually, that probably wouldn't be the issue, that would come when I had to tag the bag as evidence. She'd kill me before she'd part with her Louie. Fake and all, that thing is her most prized possession.

She gives me another whack to the head, and I make a mental note to get a CAT scan. I've taken a couple of hits in the last two weeks it's probably not a bad idea.

"I got a call from Father Murphy this morning."

"It's eight o'clock. What time did he call you?"

"Never mind that," she scolds. "He was crying."

I'm having a hard time following this story, partly because Antonia is probably freaking out in my bedroom, but also because I'm trying to understand why a priest is calling my mother early on a Sunday morning, crying when he should be preparing for mass.

"Isn't it a little too late for him to regret the vow of celibacy?"

"You broke the statue of Santa Rosalia!" she shouts before she switches to Italian and calls me everything from a disgrace to a stupid piece of donkey shit. At least I think it's a donkey. My Italian is a little sketchy. She stops in the middle of her rant and sniffs me.

Uh oh.

"What the hell is that smell?" she asks.

I scratch my cheek.

"Well, Ma, you see, before you knocked so pleasantly on my door—"

She pushes past me, and I bang my head against the door.

Definitely gonna need that CAT scan.

"Oh my God! Your kitchen was on fire? Why didn't you tell me your kitchen was on fire?" she shrieks, spinning around. Charging for me, she grabs my face. "Are you okay? You didn't suffer any burns, did you? You're too pretty."

She forces my mouth open.

"Stick your tongue out and say ah."

If only you knew where my tongue was you wouldn't be asking me to do that.

A loud bang sounds from my bedroom, and my mother drops her hands.

Thank fuck.

"Did you hear that?"

Having enough of this circus, I swipe a hand over my face and call Antonia.

"Who?"

"Come out of the bedroom," I shout. "There's someone I'd like you to meet."

God help us both.

My mother's eyes go as wide as saucers as the door to my bedroom slowly opens. Antonia creeps out of the room, fully dressed in a pair of yoga pants and the same t-shirt, her hair in a bun on top of her head. A very high bun that makes me do a double take. It looks like there's a beehive on top of her head.

"Ma, this is Antonia. Antonia, my mother, Carmella."

"It's very nice to meet you, Mrs. Pirelli," Antonia says, smiling sheepishly.

Oh, I get it.

She's going for the innocent look.

The *'I didn't just have your son's mouth on my pussy'* look.

Cute.

My mother scrutinizes Antonia for another minute before looking back at me.

"You have a girl in your apartment."

"Are you sure you're not a detective?" I ask, mildly amused.

"I was starting to wonder if you were gay."

My mouth hangs open in shock. Did she really just say that?

"What?"

"Don't what me! You're almost thirty. I should have three grandchildren by now." She slices her eyes back to Antonia. "It's so good to meet you, honey." Then the smile falls from her face and her eyes go wide again. "Father Murphy said you got into a scuffle over a girl. Is this the reason you broke the sacred saint?"

"It's a good story to tell the grandkids, no?" I retort, ignoring Antonia's red cheeks and the lethal glare she shoots my way.

"You're pregnant?"

"What? No!"

"She might be," I say thoughtfully, recalling our stint in the shower.

"For fuck's sake, I'm not pregnant! I'm on the pill," Antonia shrieks.

Hmm.

That should be a relief, and yet I find myself mildly disappointed. I guess I've officially lost my mind. Pushing the crazy thoughts out of my head, my eyes dart between the two women in my life.

"Are you religious, dear?"

"Not particularly."

"Then you don't know what a mortal sin my son just committed."

"With all due respect, it was an accident," Antonia defends.

"That saint is decades old. A timeless tradition, and now it's a pile of trash."

"Oh, please, it was ugly as shit," I say. "I've had nightmares about that thing since I was a kid."

"You're gonna have nightmares tonight when I smack you silly," my mother threatens, shoving open the window. "This place is full of smoke."

"That's my fault too," Antonia admits miserably. "I tried to cook breakfast."

My mother's head turns.

"You don't know how to cook?"

"Nope," Antonia says, smacking her lips together. "I'm not the ideal candidate for your son."

"You have a uterus, honey, you'll do."

"I really like your mom," Antonia says as she climbs into my bed.

After the smoke cleared, my mom got to work on making us a real breakfast. The two bonded over bacon and eggs and I sat there trying not to read too much into it. Not only did she fit perfectly around Tig and Delia, but she also got along with my mother even though the woman offered to track her period to determine what days she was most fertile.

Once the table was cleared, and numbers were exchanged, my mother announced she was leaving us to go to church. But before she left, she made me write her a check to replace the saint and offered me my grandmother's engagement ring to give to Antonia. By lunchtime, I was six hundred dollars poorer, horny, and on the verge of getting married.

Antonia decided we should get out of the house for a little while and so we went to the supermarket where I picked up the ingredients I needed to cook us dinner. When we got back to the apartment, I put on the Yankee game and popped open a beer. I was surprised to find out Antonia loved baseball too.

Her phone rang a few times during the game. I assumed it was her father or someone for the club, but she told me it was her mother. She got quiet after that and I asked her what was wrong. She told me her mother was the complete opposite of mine and she resented her for leaving Tank. She also revealed her mom as one of the best criminal defense lawyers in New York City and her number one client was her ex-husband.

That threw me for a loop, but I didn't say anything.

We cooked dinner together—well, I cooked. After the breakfast fiasco, I left her in charge of the salad. She couldn't set the house on fire slicing a cucumber.

Now, it's long past dinner, and I'm fucking exhausted. All I want to do is sleep and she wants to talk about my mother…*again.*

I love my mother, but no thank you.

"C'mere," I whisper, spreading my arms wide for her. She nestles against my side and leans over the nightstand to shut the lamp. "Good night," I murmur, kissing the top of her head.

"Marco?"

"Hmm?"

"Did you mean what you said yesterday?"

She's going to have to be more specific. I've said a lot of shit in the last twenty-four hours. I have had a lot of insane thoughts too.

"About coming with me to the clubhouse?" she clarifies.

My eyes spring open as she lifts her head from my chest and meets my gaze.

"To get your things?"

"If it comes down to that, but I thought you could talk to him and maybe make him understand that being a cop is just a small piece of the man you are."

I don't know that me being a cop is a small piece of anything when it comes to Tank DeLuca.

"Forget it," she says. "It's a stupid idea. Being around your mom today, made me think of him and how I wish he wasn't so stubborn…" her voice trails and she glances down at her hands, twisting the hem of her t-shirt. "I'm happy," she whispers. "These last two days have been the best days I've had in…well, a long time. But it sucks being happy and not being able to share it with the person you love most in this world." She looks back at me. "We've been fighting a lot lately and I suppose that's partially my fault. I'm not the easiest person to get along with—something you should probably know before we take this any further. When I get something in my head, I run with it. There's no changing my mind. And no one can tell me I can't do something because that word simply isn't part of my vocabulary. I'll only work ten times harder to prove I can."

"Antonia—"

"He doesn't get that…my dad."

He's a fool, a goddamn fool. If I had a daughter, I would never clip her wings. I may not agree with everything she wants or does, but I think a parent can only offer their guidance. Eventually, they need to let go. Kids are going to make mistakes. It's part of the journey. But a parent should never discourage their child to follow their hearts. They should never be told they can't try something different because that thing they don't necessarily agree with, may be the one thing that changes their whole life.

I place a finger to her lips, silencing.

"Babe, can we put the coming to Jesus moment on hold so I can answer your question?"

She nods softly.

"Since we're being open and honest, you should know a few things about me too. I don't say things I don't mean. I told you I would take you to the clubhouse and I will. You want me to talk to him, to plead my case, I'll do that too."

"You will?"

"If it makes you happy, yeah."

She throws her arms around my neck and presses a wet kiss to my lips. I smile against her mouth, realizing I mean those words with every fiber of my being.

If making nice with her dad keeps her smiling, I'm all in.

"I'll pick you up after work and we'll head over there tomorrow."

She pulls back an inch and our eyes lock.

"You're too good to be true, Pirelli."

Nah, I'm just tired and in need of a CAT scan.

CHAPTER TWENTY-ONE

ANTONIA

SPENDING THE WEEKEND WITH MARCO and meeting some of his family was bittersweet. On one hand, I was thrilled. Tig and Delia were cool as fuck and Marco's mom, Carmella, she reminded me of the actress Katherine Narducci in the movie *A Bronx Tale*. She had no filter and nothing but love for her son. All in all, Marco's family was great, and they all made me feel like I was one of them. Like I belonged.

But on the other hand, it made me miss my dad. I don't mean in the physical sense, either. I missed the relationship we used to have and the more I thought about it, the more I realized things didn't change because of my new job. They have been changing since I hit puberty. The internship was just the straw that broke the camel's back.

Fathers and daughters are tricky.

A dad is a little girl's first love. He's a consistent hero throughout her childhood. The man who scares away the monsters under the bed and kisses all her boo-boos. The guy who teaches her how to pedal a bike and the one who let's go of the seat when the training wheels are off, giving her room to fly on her own.

But something shifts when those awkward teen years show up.

The man becomes scared of the little girl. He realizes there is a clock ticking somewhere in the distance and one day he's going to have to share her. He tries to prepare himself, but nothing helps. The hands that once pushed her to fly suddenly try to pull her back.

He wishes for more time.

For a pause button.

He tries to rewind the track and all he winds up doing is breaking the one thing he tried to preserve.

My dad may do bad things, but he's still my dad.

He's still my first love.

The hero of my childhood.

This thing between me and Marco, it's not going anywhere. At least that's the impression I got this weekend and if I'm being honest, I don't want it to. For the first time in my adult life, I'm happy. There's this guy, and he's everything I never knew I wanted, and he wants me just the way I am. He's not some guy looking to climb the ranks of his club and he's not looking to put my dad behind bars either.

He's in it for me.

Just me.

A girl shouldn't have to choose between her dad and the man that makes her happy. The man she can see herself loving. The one who may be the hero of the rest of her story.

That's why I asked Marco to come with me to speak with my dad. If I could bridge the gap between us and somehow make him see Marco wasn't the enemy, then maybe my dad and I could repair all the damage adolescence left in its wake.

Being the amazing guy, he is, Marco agreed. I knew that took a lot from him too. Like my father took an oath to serve his club, Marco took an oath to protect and serve the city of New York. They would never see eye to eye on a lot of things, but Marco was willing to try, and that's all I could ask for.

After he dropped me off at work, I called my dad. He didn't answer, and that worried me. Despite our differences, we had never gone this long without speaking. I sent him a text message, telling him I would be stopping by after work and left out the fact that I would be with Marco.

It's been hours since I sent that message and still no response. I can't focus on the emails coming through because in the pit of my stomach, I know something is wrong. Normally, I'd call one of the guys to check in and make sure one of my dad's enemies didn't leave him riddled with bullets on the side of the road, but that bridge is burned.

The princess of the motorcycle club has been knocked off her chrome throne and labeled a traitor.

Sighing, I twist the paperclip I've been playing with for the last hour. My phone lights up with an incoming call and relief washes over me when I see my father's name appear on the screen. Tossing the office supplies aside, I accept the call and lift the phone to my ear.

"Dad?"

"Listen to me very carefully," he grinds out. "I know you're set on living your own life and fucking me in the process, but you need to put our shit aside and get your ass to compound immediately. Ritmo is outside waiting for you. Antonia, this is a matter of life and death. The entire club is on lockdown. There is no time for you to throw a fit or go fucking rogue on my ass. You hear me?"

I swallow hard.

There is an edge to the tone of his voice, one that I've come accustomed to. It's a sure sign he's not bluffing.

"For fuck's sake, speak!"

"Okay," I whisper hoarsely. "I'm leaving now," I say quickly and before I can disconnect the call, I'm on my feet. Slinging my bag over my shoulder, I pocket my phone. I don't bother powering off my computer, nor do I tidy up my desk. I don't even knock when I storm into Soraya's office. I tell her I have a family emergency and that I need to leave immediately.

It sounds better than saying, *hey, I gotta go. Everyone in my family is a criminal, and we're all on lockdown.*

Without giving her a chance to respond, I flee her office as quickly as my boots carry me and opt for the stairs instead of the elevator. It's quicker and time is of the essence.

When I finally reach the garage and spot Ritmo a sense of dread washes over me. It's as if my body and mind are working to warn me something terrible is about to happen.

I wish I wouldn't have dismissed it so easily.

Maybe then I would've been prepared for the moment my world came crashing down.

They say you never see the bad guys coming.

Well, I never saw the crooked cop coming.

Shame on me.

CHAPTER
TWENTY-TWO

MARCO

"How was your weekend, Pirelli?" Richie asks as he looks over the selection of donuts in the breakroom. I don't know why he bothers. The guy never strays from the Boston Cream.

Leaving him to his donut woes, I think about the question. At the risk of sounding like a total pussy, I contemplate telling him the truth. It was the best fucking weekend of my life. But that would cause the poor bastard to spit his coffee out and Judy would have my balls in a vise for ruining the donuts.

"It was great. Tig and Delia were surprised, and everyone loved Antonia, including my mother."

There, short and sweet.

So why the fuck does he still spit his coffee all over the donuts?

"You introduced her to your mother?" he admonishes, wiping the coffee from the front of his uniform.

"Judy's going to kill you, man," I point out, handing him a stack of napkins. He snatches them from me and narrows his eyes.

"Don't change the subject," he says.

"I didn't purposely introduce them," I explain with a sigh. "I took Antonia to the feast on Friday and I got into a scuffle. The Santa Rosalia statue broke and the priest who gave me my First Holy Communion decided to rat me out to my mom. She came over on Sunday to have me write a check to the church and Antonia was there."

I purposely leave out the details on how the saint broke. If I tell Richie I got into a fight with Hound and had words with Tank, I'm sure he'll have something to say and I'm not ready to deal with it. When word gets out that things between me and Antonia are serious, there's going to be talk around the department. My patience will likely be tested and my reputation as a cop may even be tarnished.

"Did your mother give her hell? God, I wish I was a fly on the wall," Richie says. "I can just picture it."

It was something that's for sure.

"Pirelli! Galante!" Judy calls.

"Shit," Richie murmurs.

"You're dead."

"Put your street clothes back on and grab your vests. Sergeant Floyd needs all hands on deck."

Richie and I exchange a look. Floyd seldom recruits us to his unit which only means something big must be going down. My guess is they're finally ready to move in on the mob case they've been building.

"Well, don't just stand there. Get a move on!"

"Yes, sir!" Richie says. "I mean Sarge…"

Stifling a laugh, I watch Judy flip him off before disappearing out of the breakroom. Turning to Richie, I loop my thumbs through my belt.

"Looks like Dinaso and Floyd are ready to put a pin in Bendetti."

"And here I thought the highlight of my day was going to be you telling me about your mom and your girlfriend," he retorts as he starts for the door.

I never thought the day would come but, I suppose he's right, Antonia is my girlfriend and if things don't work out with her father, later on, she may even be my live-in girlfriend. Talk about a mindfuck. Things are moving at lightning speed and I'm not even bothered by it.

Richie and I hurry to our lockers and change into our regular clothes. I grab my bulletproof vest and fit it to my body, securing the tabs at my chest before pulling the chain with my badge over my neck. Lastly, I check the safety on my gun and slide my piece into my holster.

A break in patrol duty is a welcome reprieve and Richie and I are eager to help. We meet the unit in the back of the precinct. However, there is no time to brief us on what's going on and we're told they will catch us up to speed on the way to the sting.

We climb into the back of the van where they wire us with recording devices and give us earpieces so that we can remain in contact with Floyd during the raid. We drive through the Brooklyn Battery Tunnel and I turn to Richie.

"Floyd didn't mention anything about Brooklyn."

"He didn't mention anything about anything. He ordered us to the van, and that's that. We can be walking into a fucking massacre for all we know," he mutters as he inches forward and focuses on the two undercover detectives in the front of the van. "Hey, you guys wanna tell us what the hell we're doing?"

"Dinaso will fill you in."

Richie quirks a brow and turns to me.

"Tony isn't even here," he mumbles.

Realizing this thing is going to eat up most of my day, I pull out my phone to call Antonia and tell her I might be late. I really hate to do that to her, especially since she's set on having me talk with her old man.

Just as I go to hit send, the van comes to a stop and the back doors swing open. Tony Dinaso jumps in, all out of breath, and parks his ass on the bench across from me and Richie.

Deciding the call to Antonia is going to have to wait, I pocket my phone and stare at my buddy as he tries to catch his breath. His eyes dart to me, and a wicked grin appears on his lips.

"Where the fuck did you come from?" Richie asks him. "And why are you smiling at Marco like that?"

"Yeah, man, it's creepy," I agree.

He points a finger at me.

"You'll be thanking me later," he says, unscrewing the cap from a bottle of water. He takes a long drink.

Good.

Maybe he's dehydrated, that would explain why he's not making any sense.

"What am I thanking you for?"

He lowers the bottle and fixes me with a pointed look.

"For giving you a chance to finish those fuckers off."

Still not grasping what he's trying to say, I look at Richie, but he just shrugs his shoulders and offers Tony another bottle of water.

"I think he's been out in the heat for too long," Richie mutters under his breath.

Tony tips his chin toward the front windshield of the van and we both follow his gaze. A gated lot comes into view. To the left, there is a large warehouse and parked in front are about three dozen motorcycles. I don't need a mirror to know my face pales, nor do I need the confirmation that comes from Tony's mouth.

"We're about to take down the Corrupt Hellraisers."

"Wait a minute," Richie says, sounding just as shocked as me. "I thought you were working on taking out Bendetti. What the fuck is this?"

"Bendetti pointed us here."

Floyd sounds in our ears, ordering us out of the van, and the sound of his voice snaps me out of my trance. I turn to Tony and grab his arm.

"I can't go in there."

"What are you talking about?" Tony asks, pulling his arm out of my reach. Before I can answer him, he kicks open the back of the cage and we're greeted by SWAT. I rush to stand in front of Tony and force his attention back to me.

"I can't fucking go in there, Dinaso, because you're about to take down my girlfriend's father," I rasp.

He narrows his eyes.

"You already went a couple of rounds with them at the feast. I thought you'd be a shoo-in for this." He pauses and closes the distance between us, poking his finger against the vest shielding my chest. "I've worked this case for six fucking months, I'm not about to throw it all down the drain because you decided to dip your dick in Hellraiser pussy. Now, put your personal shit aside, you're a fucking cop. It's your duty to put these assholes down and if you fuck up, Floyd's going to have your badge."

There's nothing I can say.

Nothing I can do.

Everything implodes.

Floyd gets on the earpiece again, and on his command, we charge into the clubhouse. Someone must've tipped them off because we're greeted with a spray of bullets.

Antonia's face flashes before me as I reach for my gun and I force myself to shake the image from my head.

Thinking of her will only get me killed, and I'd like to live to explain this mess to her.

"You motherfucker, I knew you were no good." a familiar voice sneers.

Cocking my gun, I spin around and come face to face with Hound. There's a bandage covering the bridge of his nose and he's sporting two black eyes. If he wasn't aiming a gun at me, I might take the time to admire my handy work.

Instead, I shout for him to drop his weapon and put his hands in the air.

"Fuck you," he scoffs and pulls the trigger.

I barely process what's happening. I freeze as the bullet flies and another round of gunfire goes off behind me. Hound's bullet pierces my vest, and the force knocks me back.

"Pirelli, get down," Richie shouts.

For some reason, Richie's voice registers, and I duck out of the way. He fires his gun, sending a bullet straight into Hound's chest. The gun falls from his hand as he drops to the floor and Richie rushes for me. His eyes scan the length of me, searching for a wound.

"You okay?"

"Yeah, …he got my vest," I stammer.

Around us, gunfire continues to sound. I've been trained for situations like this, and yet my mind is blank. I look back at Hound, watching as he struggles to breathe. In all the years on the job, I've been lucky never to witness death and now, I'm surrounded by it.

"Wake the fuck up, man," Richie calls, slapping the side of my face. I bring my eyes back to my partner. "He could've killed you."

He's right. None of these guys are thinking about Antonia. They don't give a fuck that she's with me, that I make her happy. They think I'm the fucking enemy and they want me dead. It's time to get my head out of my ass and do my job.

Antonia will understand.

Floyd's voice fills my ears, ordering me and Richie to make our way down the hallway.

"DeLuca's on the move," he shouts.

Richie looks at me, and I give him a quick nod.

She'll understand.

Maybe if I keep telling myself that, it will make it easier. The debilitating pain in my chest that has nothing to do with the bullet lodged in my vest, will disappear. I won't feel like I'm about to lose the one thing I give a damn about.

"I'm good," I assure him, but as I say the words, I send up a silent prayer.

Please God, don't let Tank DeLuca fire at me. I don't want to be the man who puts a bullet in Antonia's father. Putting him in cuffs and leaving his fate in the hands of the justice system is a forgivable offense. Taking his life is a death sentence to our relationship.

Richie leads me down the hallway and kicks in the door at the end open. He gives me a nod and I charge into the room with my gun aimed high. My eyes zero in on the man responsible for bringing the most beautiful girl into the world and it takes everything in me to find my voice and confront him.

"Police! Put the weapon down DeLuca and your hands in the air."

He freezes, and my pulse pounds violently in my ears, blocking out Floyd's instructions. This isn't a showdown between a cop and a criminal. This is a man falling in love, facing off against the man who made loving her possible by giving her life.

Neither one of them wants to lose her.

But both might.

Keeping his back to me he lifts both hands in the air. Richie storms in and checks the room for anyone else.

"All clear," he says, but his voice sounds so far away. My gaze drifts from the patch in the center of Tank's chest to the gun that's still in his hand.

I take two steps forward, advancing toward him and for a brief moment my mind flirts with insanity and I wish for him to turn around and pull the trigger. I guess I'd rather take a bullet than hurt Antonia and ultimately, that's how this all ends.

"I said drop your weapon," I repeat.

"Antonia."

The man doesn't fight fair.

"What about her?" I grind out.

"She's here," he reveals.

It's amazing how one piece of information can change everything. How it can send your whole fucking world crashing down. Her beautiful face flashes before me and my imagination gets the best of me as I picture her lying on the floor in a pool of blood. This is place is a fucking warzone. What if she becomes a victim?

Grinding my teeth, my hands start to shake.

"She's supposed to be at work, why the fuck is she here?" I holler at him.

Suddenly my arms feel too heavy and I start to lower my gun.

"What are you doing?" Richie growls at me.

Closing my eyes, I draw in a deep breath and force my fingers to tighten around the gun.

"Answer me," I demand. "Why the fuck is Antonia here?"

With a flick of his wrist Tank drops his gun to the floor and slowly turns to face me.

"I might be the bad guy on paper, but you're the piece of shit who toyed with an innocent girl," he sneers.

The weight of those words weighs heavily in the air because even though he's got it all wrong, that's exactly how Antonia is going to perceive this whole thing.

He knows it and so do I.

"Turn the fuck around, DeLuca," Richie hollers. "He might not put a bullet in you, but I won't fucking hesitate."

Tank ignores him and keeps his beady eyes glued to me.

"You can lock me up and throw away the key, but you better pray she comes out of this unscathed because it won't matter where I am, I will fucking ruin you."

If something happens to her, he won't have to.

I'll destroy myself.

Swallowing, I glance at Richie.

"Go find Antonia," I tell him.

"I'm not leaving you with him."

"Do it, Richie!" I yell, turning to him. My eyes plead with his. I don't need my partner to have my back, I need him to have my girls. "Please," I say hoarsely.

Go get my girl.

He hesitates for a second, before jerking his head and hurrying out of the room. Once he's gone, I turn back to Tank. We stare at each other for what seems like minutes before I lower my gun. He narrows his eyes as I tuck my gun back into my holster and reach for my handcuffs.

"Turn around," I instruct.

He contemplates the order. If he's plotting to pull a fast one on me, so be it. I don't give a fuck anymore. I'll go down as the cop who botched Sergeant Floyd's operation and still be gifted a key to the city for my efforts. Maybe DeLuca ain't that off. We live in a world fueled by corruption. It doesn't matter which side of the law you're on, there's always an out somewhere.

Perhaps I'm the weak link in this story.

"As you wish," he finally says and turns around.

I didn't realize I was holding my breath, waiting for him to make his move until I exhale and the weight on my chest subsides.

Closing the space between us, I grab his hands and slap the cuffs on him. I read him his Miranda rights and drag him out of the room. We hit the hallway and I try to focus, but all I can think about is Antonia.

Please let Richie find her.

Please let her be okay.

Entering the main room, my feet come to a halt and I take in the carnage around me. There are bodies on the floor and cops everywhere. In a sea of blue, I spot a mass of wild curls and all the air leaves my lungs as Antonia turns. Her eyes don't meet mine, though. Instead, they lock with Tanks.

"Dad?!"

He doesn't say a word, but judging by the way his shoulders slouch, I know he's just as relieved I am. Even with tears streaming down her cheeks, she's the most beautiful thing I've ever seen and when her eyes finally do find mine, I realize she's also the picture of heartbreak.

"No," she cries in disbelief.

"Antonia," I say, but my voice gets lost as Tank talks over me.

"I told you never to trust a pig," he tells her.

I flinch at his words and try to muster the courage to look her in the eye. Just when I think I can do it, Tony steps forward, blocking my view of her and takes Tank out of my custody. Antonia watches as her father is roughly dragged out of the clubhouse and I take the opportunity to make my way to her.

I reach for her hand, but she pulls it back and steps out

away from me. I meet her gaze and it's a punch to the gut. I've never seen eyes so dull and lifeless before.

"I know what you're thinking, but it's not what it looks like. I had no idea I was coming here today—"

Cutting me off, she spats, "Get away from me."

"Antonia…"

She wipes her cheeks with the backs of her hands and steps closer to me. Her dark eyes lock with mine and my heart hammers against my chest.

"I hate you," she whispers.

That's funny.

Because I could swear, I love you.

CHAPTER TWENTY-THREE

MARCO

STANDING BESIDE ME, RICHIE OFFERS me a Styrofoam cup of coffee.

"How's it going?" he questions as I tear my eyes away from the glass separating me and Antonia's father. I look down at the sludge swirling around in the cup and back at my partner.

"He won't talk," I reveal, diverting my gaze back to the glass.

Inside the interrogation room, Tank sits at a metal table handcuffed and across from Tony Dinaso who has been questioning him for the last three hours.

When we arrived at the station, I was finally clued in on what the hell was going on. As it turns out, Bendetti didn't actually lead Floyd to the Corrupt Hellraiser's. You see, even after months of investigating the notorious gangster, all their evidence is circumstantial. They got a couple of bodies they can pin on him but without his prints on the weapons or an eyewitness, Bendetti walks. That's where Tank comes in.

Tony wants him to testify and say he sold the guns to Bendetti. At least that's what I got from this whole fucking thing. I wasn't paying all that much attention to the briefing, I was too busy licking my wounds over Antonia.

After she told me she hated me, she told me she wished she'd never met me. Then she wished me death and told me to fucking burn in hell. It became clear she wasn't going to give me a chance to explain myself anytime soon and so, here I am…miserable and watching her father be questioned.

I've lost count of how many times he's spit in Dinaso's face.

The man is a fucking savage.

"You know she's downstairs, right?" Richie supplies, taking a sip of his coffee. I tear my eyes away from Tank and Dinaso's pissing match to eye my partner. I had a feeling she would come here. It's not like she had many options, the people she considers family are either here in a holding cell or on a slab in the morgue. I wonder if she realizes that.

Swallowing, I look back at the glass.

"Is she okay?" I ask.

"You could go find out for yourself."

I shake my head. I'm the last thing she needs.

Ironic considering that's all I want to be.

How any of this happened, I'll never understand.

I wasn't supposed to fall for her.

Suddenly, Tony's voice booms over the speaker, and Floyd appears in front of the glass.

"Pirelli, you're up."

"What's he talking about?" I ask, turning to Richie.

Floyd knocks on the glass and signals me for me to join the room.

"Looks like DeLuca wants you," Richie says.

Great.

I can't wait to see how this goes.

Sighing, I hand Richie my coffee cup and make my way to the interrogation room. Floyd opens the door and brushes past me, cursing Tank under his breath. For the guy in charge, he's doing an awful job at instructing us. This isn't my case. I've got a fucking stack of tickets I could be inputting into the system. Instead, I'm walking into the lion's den.

Closing the door behind me, I cross my arms against my chest and look expectantly at Tony. Perhaps he can clue me in on what the fuck I'm supposed to do now.

"This son of a bitch won't budge," Tony grunts.

"How many times do I gotta tell you, I ain't no fucking rat," Tank sneers.

"You're gonna die like a rat in a cage if you don't start talking," Tony volleys, pushing off his chair. Grabbing his files from the table, he tucks them under his arm and tips his chin toward me. I follow him out of the room and lean against the door.

"Get him to give up Bendetti," he says, pointing a finger at me.

My eyes widen at the ridiculous demand. I'm the last person Tank is going to give a statement to.

"What makes you think he's going to talk to me?"

"He requested to speak to you."

"That's because he wants to kill me."

"He's handcuffed to a chair," Tony retorts. "Unless you sit on his lap, you're safe. Now, go and maybe I can convince Floyd not to report you to internal affairs."

As far as I'm concerned, I did my job. There are no

grounds for me to be written up, but I don't get a chance to question Tony because he turns and walks away from me.

Cursing him, Floyd, and the whole department, I drag my fingers roughly through my hair and push the door to the interrogation room open. Stepping inside, I kick it closed. I don't meet Tank's gaze right away. Instead, I stalk across the room. Balling my fists, I roll my neck and stare at our reflections in the two way glass.

"Rough day?" Tank questions nonchalantly.

Like I said, the man's a savage.

A brutal fucking savage.

Turning around, I cock my head to the side and glare at him.

"You could say that," I grind out.

"I imagine it's taxing breaking the heart of a young woman for the sake of an arrest," he says pointedly.

"Probably just as challenging as breaking the heart of your only child for the sake of a patch," I reply evenly and move to take the seat across from him.

Folding myself into the chair, I stare at him.

We're two men divided by difference.

I'm a man baptized in boundaries.

He's the man schooled in sin.

Our only common thread is the woman we both failed.

"Tell me something, officer—I can call you that, right?" I don't reply, and he continues. "Do you want children someday?"

I have no idea where he's going with this, but I'm pretty sure I ain't going to pull a statement out of him if we keep shooting the shit like a bunch of broads at a beauty parlor.

"I didn't want kids," he reveals. "I knew my lifestyle wasn't suited for children. But the man upstairs had a different plan for me." He pauses and smiles faintly before continuing, "The moment I found out Antonia's mother was pregnant, something changed inside of me. I wanted to be better. I wanted to be worthy of such a gift, but I had already made my bed. I took an oath and signed my life away, and I couldn't erase that just because I had gotten my girl knocked up. No one was going to give me a pardon. You see, there's a line. You're sitting on one side of it and I'm sitting on the other. You can cross over to my side but I can't cross back to yours because if I ever did, my daughter would pay the price and no child should ever have to suffer for the sins of their father."

His eyes narrow as he leans forward.

"You did a shitty thing using my daughter to get to me, but your plan backfired because I ain't giving anyone up. A lot of blood has touched my hands, but my daughter's will never be on them."

"I'm only going to say this one more time, so listen up, old man, I didn't use your daughter. I pulled Antonia over a couple of weeks ago because she's a piss poor driver. Tell me, did she get that from you?" I don't let him answer the question as I continue, mimicking his stance by leaning over the table too. "I was prepared to pick up Antonia from work and bring her to your place. She wanted me to talk to you, to make you see what she sees in me."

"All I see is a crooked cop who took advantage of my daughter."

I take it back.

He's no savage.

He's a thickheaded son of a bitch with an anger problem.

"Look closer," I tell him. "You'll see a man who cares about her. I didn't plan on your daughter. I didn't want to share my life with anyone, but the way her existence changed you, it changed me too. I don't have enemies."

"You're looking at one."

"Because I came to work and did my job? Is that what makes me your enemy?"

He opens his mouth to speak, but I hold up a hand.

"I'm a cop and a mediocre one. That's my only offense, DeLuca. If it wasn't me who put those cuffs on you today, it would've been someone else. Another cop, probably a better one too. Arresting you would've been the highlight of his career."

"Why not yours?"

"Because there's a woman downstairs who is hurting because of all this and my career doesn't seem all that important knowing that I had a hand in that. You got a choice here, Tank. You can keep your mouth shut and take the wrap for the guns, but with your record you're looking at fifteen years. Let me not forget the charges they're going to tack on from today. They got you assaulting a police officer with a deadly weapon and newsflash, one of our guys is in critical condition from a gunshot wound to the neck. If he doesn't make it—"

"I get it," he interrupts. "Doesn't change anything."

"Give them Bendetti and I'll get them to cut you a deal. Five years. If you stay out of trouble, you might even be eligible to get out on an early release."

I have no fucking idea if any of this is feasible.

I'm like a fucking magician.

For my next act, I'll pull a probation deal out of my hat.

Tank laughs wickedly in my face, and I grimace.

Yeah, man, I don't buy my bullshit either.

But you can't blame a guy for trying.

"You said yourself you're a mediocre cop," he points out.

About that…it seemed like a good thing to say at the time.

Now, not so much.

"I'm a mediocre cop, but I'm a good guy," I say, and he raises an eyebrow.

Well, you got his attention.

Don't drop the ball, dickhead.

"I'm a good guy who loves your daughter," I blurt.

"You barely know my daughter," he scoffs.

"How long did it take you to fall in love with her?"

"Seconds."

"Then you know it's possible," I say, pausing for a beat. "Take the deal Tank, and I'll take care of Antonia."

It would be my pleasure.

CHAPTER TWENTY-FOUR

ANTONIA

SEEING MY FATHER BE DRAGGED out of the clubhouse in a pair of cuffs wasn't all that shocking to me. It was normal and if I'm being honest, a relief. It meant his enemies hadn't caught up to him. It meant one of the bodies on the floor wasn't his.

It meant there was still time to make things right between us.

He had spent most of his life beating the charges brought against him; I had no doubt he'd beat whatever they were hitting him with now too. Albeit, I don't recall a time when SWAT was involved, but my dad was alive, and I had faith.

For about a second.

Then my eyes drifted to the man responsible for the shiny cuffs decorating my dad's wrists. The man I trusted, the one who swore he wasn't like the others that came before him. The man I thought I could love and would love me in return. Marco was supposed to restore my heart, not break it beyond repair.

There is nothing I hate more than being made the fool, and that's exactly what I am. A stupid fucking fool who was so thirsty for love and affection, she let her guard down and invited the enemy to her front door. Those bodies I mentioned, all that carnage—I did that.

Me and my foolish heart are the culprits.

And if my dad never sees the light of day again, that's on me too.

The sound of heels clicking against the linoleum floor catches my attention and I lift my head, spotting their owner immediately. She sticks out like a sore thumb, perfectly posh and filthy rich. I bet those shoes cost more than my Harley.

"Antonia," she exclaims, rushing for me.

Don't roll your eyes,

You need her to get your dad out of this mess you created.

"Mom," I reply curtly as I rise to my feet. Her eyes slowly rake over me, and a slightly horrified expression settles on her face.

"What happened to you?"

"I'm having a rough day. Can we maybe skip the judgments?"

"I didn't mean it that way," she argues. "You've been crying."

Someone polish a trophy for her.

"Yeah, because the only parent who gives a damn about me is currently in a cell and the men who helped him raise me are either dead or in a jail cell next to his."

I close my eyes, wishing the truth wasn't so harsh.

The world a little less ugly.

I will not cry in front of her.

Drawing in a deep breath, I ignore the hurt reflected in

her eyes. She doesn't get to feel bad. She walked away from all of this, and she'll walk away again.

"My dad pays you a lot of money, keeping you in those designer heels of yours. Earn them and keep him out of jail."

She doesn't make a move and I lose my patience with her. My gaze darts around the crowded precinct until it settles in on the cranky old desk sergeant who stole my melons. Brushing past my mother, I march toward her, recalling my last visit here and the pack of cigarettes I caught her pocketing. Before I can ask the broad if I can bum a cigarette from her, I hear a familiar voice call my name.

A voice that belongs to a man I wish didn't exist.

"Antonia," Marco repeats.

As if I didn't fucking hear him the first time.

"We need to talk," he says.

The man is clueless. If the world was burning to ash, and he was the last man standing, I wouldn't waste my spit on him much less speak to him.

"Look, I know what you're thinking, but—"

Something inside me snaps and I turn around. Blinded by rage, I don't even look at him as I rear my fist back and clock him in the jaw. His hand moves to his cheek and the entire precinct comes to a standstill as he stares at me with a look of defeat in those expressive eyes of his.

"You have no idea what I'm thinking!" I shriek. "I told you to leave me the fuck alone, and I meant it. I don't want to see you. I don't want to talk to you…" my words trail as I shake out my throbbing fingers. "And there's plenty more where that came from so if you're smart, you'll fuck off somewhere."

He drops his hand from his cheek and squares his shoulders.

Why is he still standing here?

"I'm not going anywhere until you hear me out. I spoke to your father—"

A shrill scream leaves my lips as I plug my fingers into my ears and tune him out. He can take his excuses and shove them where the sun doesn't shine. When his lips finally stop moving, I remove my fingers from my ears and turn my back to him. The desk sergeant stares at me as if I've lost my mind and I'm starting to wonder if I have.

"I know you smoke," I begin. "I saw you with a pack of cigarettes the other day."

"What's your point?"

"My point is, I'm sort of having a nervous breakdown and could really use a cigarette right now."

She blinks in response, and I huff out an exasperated breath.

"You stole my edible fruit arrangement lady, the least you can do is let me bum a cigarette off you."

"You just assaulted one of my officers."

"Great, so lock me up. It's what you people do best around here," I seethe, slamming my fist against the counter. "You know what? Keep your fucking cigarette."

There's a bodega on the corner and I need to get the hell out of here. I go to make my way out of the precinct when Marco grabs my hand. Shockingly, I don't pull away from his touch. Instead, my gaze wanders to our joined hands.

I really wanted that hand to be the one I held for the rest of my life.

"I'm not the bad guy here, Antonia," he murmurs. "Give me a chance to make it right."

My eyes drift back to his, and I finally pull away from him.

"No, you're not the bad guy. You're worse than that."

The tears I was trying so hard not to shed, slip from the corners of my eyes and I don't make an attempt to hide them from him. I glance around the precinct, looking for my mom, but she's nowhere in sight and my heart cracks a little more. I truly have no one.

A whimper escapes my lips, and I rush out of the precinct. I make it halfway down the stairs before I totally lose it. Sobbing, I drop onto the steps, defeated.

I should've known this is how it would end.

I should've built walls around my heart.

I should've feared love.

I should've realized happily ever after doesn't really exist.

I have no idea how long I sit there crying, feeling sorry for myself, but when there are no more tears left to cry, I lift my head and notice the sun has gone down. Pulling myself together, I wipe my eyes and glance back at the police station. The doors push open, and my mother steps outside, her eyes immediately finding mine. She closes the distance between us and sets her briefcase down on the steps. Without saying a word, she pulls me into her arms, and I go completely still.

I don't remember the last time my mother hugged me.

The scent of her perfume wafts past my nose and I feel my throat tighten. For a long time, I struggled to recall her scent. To recall the way her hands felt on my hair. Even her laugh. I don't know if I'm vulnerable or what the case is, but I need this hug and maybe I need my mother too.

"No matter what happens, you're going to be just fine. You're not alone," she murmurs against my hair.

My brows pinch together, and I untangle myself from her arms.

"Does that mean you can't get him off this time?"

Sighing, she cocks her head to the side.

"They offered your father a deal and I've told him to take it." She pauses to shake her head. "Antonia, your father has been playing Russian roulette with the law for thirty years. If he doesn't take the deal, he's looking at a minimum of fifteen years and though I am a damn good lawyer, I don't think I can sweep this one under the rug."

"You didn't even try," I accuse.

"It's too risky," she insists. "I am not confident he gets out of this without doing time. Now, we can roll the dice and hope he's out in fifteen, but let's call a spade a spade, Antonia, fifteen years will kill your father. This way he's out in five."

I shake my head.

I haven't had to live a day without him, how am I supposed to survive five years?

"I know this is a lot to take in, but Tank already agreed. We're just waiting on the district attorney to get the paperwork together and then we'll go in front of the judge."

"That's it?" I admonish. "We're just going to let him go to jail?"

She doesn't reply.

I guess that's my answer.

"Come on, I'll take you home," she says.

There's no fight left in me and so I let her lead me away from the precinct, but it feels like I'm leaving a piece of me behind.

It's okay.

Who needs a treacherous heart, anyway?

CHAPTER TWENTY-FIVE

ANTONIA

I ONCE HEARD SOMEONE SAY if you follow a spiral inward, it never ends. It will just keep tightening infinitely. I think that's what happened; I followed the spiral and there's no magic lever to release the pressure. I can't claw my way to the top or reverse the damage.

After my mother drove me home, I passed out on the couch. I don't know if she stayed with me, but by the time I woke up; she was gone. I was glad because I wasn't in the mood or the frame of mind to deal with anyone.

That didn't stop the phone from ringing, though, or the infinite text messages from Marco, which I ignored. I think the only reason I didn't bury my phone in the backyard was that I was still holding out for a miracle. Still hoping my dad would call me and tell me to pick him up, that the charges were dropped, and he was a free man.

But that didn't happen.

Soraya called and left a message. She left several messages actually and at first, they were work related.

Hey, I'm just calling to check in. I hope you were able to take care of that family emergency.

An hour later…

You're later than usual, is everything okay?

Twenty minutes after that.

Ok, I guess you're not coming in today. Can you at least give me a call and let me know if you're okay? You left really abruptly yesterday.

Five minutes later…

I just got off the phone with Marco. Call me.

The last message she sent was a response to the anonymous submission I had sent to her last week. I couldn't bring myself to read it. Just knowing that she knew it was me who had sent it was enough to send me over the edge. I grabbed whatever I could find in my dad's liquor cabinet and started drinking.

It was five o'clock somewhere and if it wasn't, I didn't care. When your life falls to shit, there isn't a manual to follow. Etiquette isn't a concern. You just roll with the punches and hope you survive the day.

When it did actually become five o'clock, my phone dinged with a calendar alert. I had forgotten all about my scheduled appointment with Tig. Instead of dismissing the alert like I should have, I pulled open my rideshare app. I was too drunk to drive, but I decided I wasn't going to miss the appointment. A tattoo was the furthest thing from my mind. I just wanted to know if everything was a lie. Did Tig really want to meet me or was he part of the plan too? In my drunken stupor, I even wondered if Marco lied about Tig and Delia's infertility issues. It didn't seem that much of a stretch when I had already convinced myself the only reason Soraya hired me in the first place was to assist Marco in his agenda to take down my dad.

My ride arrived in ten minutes and now, a half hour later, I'm standing outside Tig's shop in the rain, holding an empty bottle of Jack Daniels, wondering how the fuck I let any of this happen. I'm about to turn around and leave when Tig's eyes meet mine through the glass window. He rises from his stool and makes his way toward the door. Opening it, he steps outside and pulls the hood of his sweatshirt over his head.

"I didn't think you were going to show," he says over the rain.

I blink the rain away from my eyelashes and swallow. Coming here was another mistake.

"I'm sorry…" I stammer, glancing down at the empty bottle in my hand. Tears well in my eyes and I feel myself start to break. Tig takes the bottle from my hand and lifts my chin with his finger.

"Come inside," he says.

I know I shouldn't, but I let him lead me into the shop. He nods for me to take a seat at his station and shrugs his hoodie from his shoulders. Draping it over the front desk, he chucks the bottle of Jack and reaches under the desk to open a cabinet, pulling out a bottle of Patron. I watch him walk to the door and flick the sign that reads 'we're open' to 'we're closed'.

My mind flashes back to the night Marco shared Tigs story with me and how he said they were hurting financially from all the fertility treatments. He made me understand that Tig and Delia didn't miss a day of work, nor did they close their shop for no good reason. Yet, there's no sign of Delia, and Tig just closed his doors.

Lies.

They're everywhere.

"Were you in on it too?" I blurt the question and he turns to face me. Unscrewing the cap from the bottle of Tequila, he straddles his stool and offers it to me. He's about to stomp on what's left of my heart, I'd be a fool not to drink his booze.

"I don't know what you're talking about," he says as I knock back the tequila. It slides smoothly down my throat, so I take another sip.

Tig takes the bottle from me before I can get a third shot in and I sneer at him.

"Don't pretend like you don't know what happened. He's your cousin."

"There are two sides to every story and I only know one," he replies, setting the bottle on the counter next to his tattoo gun.

"Hey, I wasn't done with that," I say, pointing to the bottle.

"Yeah, you are," he says, crossing his arms against his chest. "If you don't want to be the one who does the talking, then I'll do the talking and you do the listening."

I didn't come here for a pep talk; I came here so he could reveal all the horrible lies his cousin let me believe and I can finally be done with him.

"I knew you were special by the way he talked about you when he was here, that's why I wanted to meet you myself. There's not much that rattles Marco, but you shook his whole fucking world and on Saturday, he was the happiest I've ever seen him. He wanted it to work with you whether you believe it or not."

"He used me to get to my father," I snap.

"That's bullshit, Antonia. Maybe that's what your dad wanted to believe himself, but it's not the case."

That makes no sense.

"Why would my dad want to believe that?"

"Because it's easier to point a finger than to take the blame."

I let those words sink in and rack my foggy brain trying to recall if there was a time in my life where my dad owned his sins, but I fall short.

"Look, I don't know your old man, but it seems like he's made some choices in his life that are tied to some pretty big consequences."

It wasn't all that long ago that I thought the same thing. In fact, it was the argument I used against him when I got the job at "Ask Ida," and I probably would've used it again had I brought Marco to the clubhouse as planned.

I won't deny the fact my father is a man who has done more bad than good. He's hurt people and torn families apart. He's broken the law and gotten away with it more times than any one person should ever be allowed. But he's my dad and while he's made a mess of his life, it's me who failed him.

"He made a career being a criminal," Tig continues. "Prison might as well be his retirement plan."

"Maybe so, but if I would've listened to him, if I would've stayed away from Marco—"

"He'd still be in a cell, only he'd be looking at fifteen years and not five."

"What are you talking about?"

"The deal your father took was Marco's idea."

"My mother, his attorney, worked out that deal with the district attorney," I argue.

"Your mother looked over the deal, sweetheart," he reveals. "Listen, let's say Marco didn't go to work yesterday —let's say you and him played hooky and stayed home all day. You think that's going to stop the department from taking down a criminal? Every man with a badge would've raided that clubhouse regardless, and everything would have played out exactly the way it did. Except your father wouldn't have asked to speak to Marco, and Marco wouldn't have convinced him to work with the cops."

He almost had me until that last line. There is no way in hell my father is voluntarily cooperating with anyone. Least alone, Marco.

"If that's the story Marco told you—"

"Marco doesn't lie to me, Antonia. If you would just hear him out, you'd realize he is the noblest guy you'll ever meet. If you don't believe me, ask your father."

"My father would never agree with that."

"You sure about that?" he asks, arching an eyebrow.

"Are you seriously telling me my father doesn't believe Marco set him up? That he wasn't using me?"

"I'm telling you your father trusts Marco enough to take the deal and leave his daughter in his capable hands." He pauses and shakes his head. "You don't see it, do you?"

"I'm a little drunk…"

"He's in love with you, Antonia, and it's fucking killing him that you think he would intentionally hurt you." He roughs a hand over his cheek before pinning me with a look. "Do you know he sat outside your house all night in case one of your father's enemies decided to show up? Not as a cop. He didn't have his badge or his gun on him. He was there as a man and he protected what's his."

It was a lot to absorb.

The declaration of love.

The revelation that Marco considered me his.

My dad putting his trust in a cop.

It was all too much, and it was everything I wanted to hear. Tears roll down my cheeks as I stare back at Tig.

"He told you he loved me?"

Muttering a curse, he drops his hand from his cheek and shakes his head.

"You're a pain in the ass, you know that?"

"Does that mean you're not giving me a tattoo?"

"It means I'm taking you home to Marco and he can answer that question himself."

My treacherous heart betrays me once again because I don't argue with Tig. I want everything he's saying to be true. I want to obliterate the line that separates us.

But most of all, I want Marco's love.

CHAPTER

TWENTY-SIX

MARCO

I**T TURNS OUT SCORING THE** deal for Tank wasn't as hard as I expected it to be. Tank had more on Bendetti than Floyd or Tony figured and when Tank told Floyd he had proof, that Bendetti killed his young son, Floyd became putty in his Tank's hand. Not only was he able to negotiate his sentence with the district attorney, but he also managed to get them to drop the charges on his VP, Cash, something I found out when Cash showed up at Antonia's house this morning and told me to get lost.

After Tank and I came to an understanding of our own, his hotshot lawyer showed—or should I say Antonia's mom arrived ready to turn shit up. I left them to work out the details of his deal and went downstairs to speak with Antonia. Not only did I want to make things right with her and explain myself, but I also wanted to tell her Tank had given us his blessing.

He didn't give me a handshake and welcome me into

the family with open arms. That wasn't his style. Instead, he threatened to maim me if I went against my word to protect his daughter.

If you hurt her, it won't matter where I am, I'll see to it you're dead.

It was very heartwarming and made me feel all warm and fuzzy inside—not.

Anyway, when I found Antonia, she still wanted no part of me, and she made it very clear by delivering a right hook to my face.

I know, I know.

I've gotten my ass kicked more in the last two weeks than I have in all my years on this earth.

Whatever, man.

Sometimes we gotta take a little pain with our pleasure.

Nothing great ever comes easy.

That's why I drove to her house as soon as I left the station and sat outside all night. She wouldn't answer my calls, but I couldn't leave her to herself. I could give her space, but if one of Tank's enemies got wind of what was going on, they might see her as a target, and no one was going to touch her on my watch. She was mine now whether she knew it or not and I take care of what's mine.

Cash showed a little after eight in the morning and briefed me a little on how things work in the Corrupt Hellraiser's world. Since it didn't look like Antonia was going to talk to me anytime soon, I left Cash at the house. I don't know if he got through to her, though.

I don't know anything.

She's still not answering my calls or even Soraya's calls.

She didn't show up for work, but I didn't expect her to.

And when I drove by her house, it was pitch dark. There was no sign of any of the Corrupt Hellraisers either. I'm giving her until eight o'clock to come to her senses. If she doesn't call me back or at least text me, I'm going to search all of fucking New York until I find her. I'm going to throw her over my shoulder and handcuff her to my bed. One way or another, the girl is going to hear me out and after I tell her the entire truth, I'm going to tell her she's stuck with me.

If she doesn't like it, too bad.

She shouldn't have made me go and fall in love with her.

The doorbell rings, jarring my attention away from the digital clock I've been staring at for the last hour. I glance at my door and back at the clock. Look at her coming to her senses with two minutes to spare.

I jump off the couch and hurry to my door. Instead of it being Antonia on the other side, it's Tig.

"Christ, you look like shit," he mutters as he drinks me in.

"In case you didn't get the memo, I'm not really in the mood for you," I tell him.

I'm about to shut the door in his face, but he wedges his boot in the doorway and shoves the door wide open with the palm of his hand. Grabbing the front of my shirt with the other hand, he pulls me out of my apartment.

"Hey, what the fuck are you doing?"

"You think you're the only one who's having a rough night? I've had my hands full for the last two hours. Now, I'd appreciate it if you collected your belongings from the back of my truck so I can get the hell home to my wife."

"My belongings? What the hell are you talking about?"

Not bothering with a reply, he turns and starts for the stairs. I follow him down the three flights and out the door. He walks to his truck parked at the curb and opens the backseat. Stepping to the side, he waves a hand.

"She's all yours, pal."

My eyes narrow as they move from him to the beauty sprawled across his backseat.

"Careful, she's thrown up three times since we left the shop," he adds.

Hurrying to the truck, I grit my teeth.

"What the hell did you do to her?"

"Hey, she was already three sheets to the wind when she got to the shop. I just gave her a little Tequila to get her talking. You're welcome, by the way."

I look back to Antonia. He wasn't exaggerating about the throw up. She reeks and I'm pretty sure she's got some in her hair. I gather her in my arms and lift her out of the backseat. Tig shuts the door and rushes to my apartment building. He holds the door for me and follows me upstairs. Once I've got her safely in my apartment, he leaves.

Unsure what to do with her, I contemplate my options. I can lay her down on my bed and let her sleep it off, but she's a mess. A shower it is. I take three steps before she starts to stir in my arms. She slowly opens her eyes and tries to lift her head from my shoulder.

"Marco?"

"Shhh," I whisper. "It's okay. I've got you now."

I don't know if those words soothe her or if she's too tired to argue, but her head drops back to my shoulder and I fight the urge to kiss her. You don't realize how empty your arms have been until you hold your world in them.

Reaching the bathroom, I gently set her on the counter. She lifts her head and I push the hair away from her face. Cupping her cheeks, I stare at her.

"Look at me," I coax softly.

Tears slide down her cheeks as those beautiful brown eyes peer back at me. The last time they were on me, they were filled with anger, pain, and even hate. Now, they're just sad.

So fucking sad.

"My dad is going to prison, Marco."

Swallowing, I thumb her tears away and nod.

"It's not your fault," she whispers.

Relief swarms me, and I go to kiss her, but her face suddenly pales. Reaching out, she fists my shirt and lurches forward. Before I can ask her what's wrong, she hurls all over me. It takes me a second to process what's happening, but instead of pushing her away, I find myself wrapping my arms around her and smoothing a hand down her back.

"Let it out," I whisper. "I got you."

From this day forward.

I've got you.

I USED TO LOOK AT other couples like Tig and Delia, Richie and Tina, even Graham and Soraya, and think they were fools. Sure, they looked happy and all that, but to be tied to one person for the rest of your life seemed like overkill to me. Then I'd listen to Tig talk about Delia, and I saw the love in his eyes. The admiration and respect he had for her took over his whole face when he spoke of her and sometimes, I wondered how something like that happens to a man.

How does a man go from only caring about himself to living simply to love someone else?

One day you're dreaming of fast cars and trips to Vegas, the next you're watching the woman you love sleep in your bed. Your mind wanders, but it's not Ferraris and showgirls that consume your thoughts. It's her in a big white dress and three kids climbing into your bed on a Sunday morning. It's holidays and trips to Disney. It's fighting over the outstanding bills but making up before you both climb into bed because you made a promise to never go to sleep angry. It's the long nights you spend loving her between the sheets and the late mornings you hold her tight. It's the times you find yourself in a crowded room, staring at her, wondering how the fuck you got so lucky.

One day you get the answer to your question and you learn it just happens. There is no rhyme or reason. When the right person comes along, you wave your white flag high and surrender your soul. You let love in.

You get a fucking CAT scan too.

You know, just to be sure you're not losing your fucking mind.

Safety first, guys!

"It wasn't a dream."

The sound of her groggy voice pulls me away from my thoughts and I focus on the beauty in my arms.

"What wasn't?"

"You."

She stares at me for a beat before she closes her eyes and groans miserably.

"Why does it feel like there's a mariachi band in my head?"

Suppressing a laugh, I smooth a hand over the top of her head.

"You hit the bottle a little too hard last night and showed up at Tig's tattoo shop. He brought you here."

"I remember that," she says, opening her eyes. "I also remember throwing up in his truck three times. Oh God, he must hate me."

"Impossible," I reply, and she turns her head. Our eyes lock, and she reaches out to touch a hand to my cheek. "You want me to get you some Tylenol?"

She shakes her head, gently rubbing her thumb back and forth over my skin.

"Tig told me what you did."

Confused, I raise an eyebrow. She's going to have to be more specific because I've done a lot of shit.

"You helped my dad get the deal."

Drawing out a sigh, I cover her hand with mine.

"I tried to tell you," I start, pausing to intertwine our fingers. Bringing our joined hands to my lips, I brush a kiss across her knuckles. "Antonia, I didn't know what was going to happen yesterday. The sergeant in charge needed extra hands, and he ordered me and my partner to change into our street clothes. We weren't even briefed until we were pulling into the compound and as soon as I realized what we were doing, I tried to get out of it. I explained that all to your father, and I also explained that I love you. I realized it when I was standing in front of your father, asking him to lower his weapon. I had the sergeant in my ear, giving me permission to shoot, but I couldn't do it. I wouldn't do it. Faced with a choice, my job, or you, I choose you. I know it didn't look that way when you saw me taking your father out of there with cuffs, but I swear—"

She cuts me off.

"I believe you," she whispers, her eyes full of tears. "I'm sorry for all the things I said and for punching you."

"Nice right hook," I tease, trying to lighten the mood. It works because she gives me a small smile. But it quickly fades, and her expression grows serious.

"What happens now?"

If there was ever a loaded question, I'm pretty sure that's it.

"Well, for starters, we're going to get showered and dressed and get our asses down to the courthouse because your father is going in front of the judge in an hour. Before they take him to Rykers, you're going to talk to him and I'm going to be right by your side."

The dam breaks and the tears fall as I continue.

"Then we're going to come home and I'm going to take care of you. We'll take it one day at a time. No more doubts. No running from one another. Lean on me, Antonia, give me your trust and let me love you because it's all I want to do."

Today, tomorrow, every fucking day until I die.

I just want to love her.

"You have five minutes," Antonia's mom says, her eyes darting between Tank and their daughter. She steps away, giving them their privacy, but I don't follow her lead. I promised I'd be by Antonia's side and unless she tells me otherwise, that's where I'll remain.

"So, this is it," Antonia whispers as she stares at her father.

"For now," he says hoarsely. "We don't have much time so I'm going to cut straight to chase. I don't want you to be sad, Tonia. I don't want you to spend these next five years crying over me. I'll be fine, especially knowing you're out here living the life you want." He pauses to swallow and looks down at his shackled hands. "I shouldn't have given you crap about that job of yours and I shouldn't have doubted your judgment," he says as he lifts his head and looks at me. "I was wrong."

He turns back to Antonia.

"Of all the men—"

"I know, I know," she whispers. "He's a cop."

"Of all the men, you found the one worthy," he says. His gaze slices back to me. "Don't make me eat my words, officer."

"I won't," I rasp. "You have my word."

He nods and focuses his attention back to his daughter.

"I love you, sweetheart. More than anything in this world." His voice cracks, and his eyes fill with water. "Never forget that."

Antonia lets go of my hand and rushes toward Tank, throwing her arms around his neck. As she hugs him his wrists strain against the metal digging into his flesh. I turn to the bailiff. Pulling my badge from under my shirt, I flash it at him.

"He's not a flight risk, undo the cuffs."

"Officer—"

"Let the man hug his daughter," I grind out, clenching my jaw tight.

He mumbles something under his breath and moves to Tank. Antonia pulls away from her father and turns around, her eyes questioning mine. I tip my chin and she diverts her attention to the bailiff, watching as he removes the cuffs from her father's wrists. Tank closes the distance between them, but instead of hugging, he lifts his hands to her face and traces every angle.

He brings her face closer and presses his lips to her forehead. The tears he was holding fall freely as he wraps his arms around her.

I'm a man who didn't realize how empty his arms were until he held the world in them, and Tank is a man who, until now, didn't realize how full his were. Two men divided by difference yet bound by one woman we consider our world.

Tank opens his eyes and looks at me.

"Thank you," he rasps.

I nod, but I really should be the one paying thanks here.

Without Tank, there would be no Antonia, and my arms would still be empty.

———

"ARE YOU OKAY?" I ASK ONCE WE LEAVE THE COURTHOUSE.

"No, but I will be," she says, wrapping her arms around my waist. "Thank you for what you did in there."

"Just evening the score a little," I murmur, bending my head to press my lips to hers.

Her body melds with mine and I let my mouth linger on hers for a moment. It's only been a few days, but I missed this.

"Hey," she says, pulling back an inch.

Her eyes meet mine as she pulls her lower lip between her teeth. Even with her eyes swollen from all the crying she's been doing, she still manages to steal my breath.

One day you wake up and it just happens.

There's no rhyme.

No reason.

You wave that white flag and you surrender.

"So, not too long ago, I went on a date with this cop," she says, releasing her lip and tightening her arms around my waist. "He took me to this little hole in the wall restaurant not too far from here, where they make the best meatball sandwiches and he talked dirty to me and promised to fuck me like a gentleman."

"Sounds like a catch."

"Oh, he is, and you know what the best part was? It turns out he's a man of his word."

"Fucked you like a gentleman, did he?" I tease, watching as she tosses her head back and laughs. It takes her a minute to sober up, but when she does, her beautiful smile is still intact.

"Yeah, he did," she says softly. "Turns out he really is a good guy."

A good guy who still plans on taking those meatballs to go so he can fuck her like the gentleman he is.

EPILOGUE

MARCO

"DID THE EDIBLE FRUIT ARRANGEMENT get there yet?" I ask.

Soraya huffs out an exasperated breath through the line. I've been torturing her since early this morning, calling the office and her cell. I'm willing to bet the first thing she does tonight when she gets home is dye her hair whatever shade means angry as fuck these days.

"For the fifth time, I will call you when the fucking fruit arrives. Now, stop calling me, Pirelli."

"It's not fruit, it's melon."

The line goes dead and I turn back to Tig.

"It still didn't get there yet. Should I call the place again?"

"Sure, if you want them to spit all over your pineapples."

Unlike Soraya, Tig won't dye his hair when he goes home, but have no fear, he hates me too. Oh, well, it's not every day a man proposes. They'll all get over it.

Pocketing my phone, I look at the velvet display board in front of me and go back to studying the three engagement rings. For the last two hours, I've been trying to decide which one will look perfect on Antonia's finger.

"This is fucking ridiculous, man," Tig says. "Pick a

damn ring, odds are you're gonna be back here on your fifth wedding anniversary resetting the damn thing anyway."

Ignoring him, I reach for the solitaire again. Originally, I came here determined to get her a princess cut ring. Then the jeweler mentioned a halo setting, and we added that style to the mix. But I keep going back to this one. It's simple and not as flashy as the other two. I think it will look perfect on her dainty finger.

"This is the one," I exclaim.

"Thank you, Jesus," Tig mutters, glaring at the jeweler. "Well, don't just stand there! Ring him up before he changes his mind. And while you're at it, take these other ones and put them away," he says, shoving the velvet board toward him.

"For someone who won a bet, you're awfully cranky."

"I didn't win shit," he argues.

"You said we'd be ring shopping in three months and here we are."

"Must be my lucky day. Do me a favor? When you two decide to have kids, lose my number. I don't want to be anywhere near you when you're trying to decide what the hell to name them."

Three months ago, I would've been struggling with how to respond because I wouldn't want to say the wrong thing and be insensitive to his and Delia's infertility situation. But God works in mysterious ways and usually when you lose hope is when you get your miracle. Tig and Delia found out last month their little miracle is on the way and in seven months, I'll be sitting in the hospital, waiting for Tig to come out of the delivery room with a big grin on his face.

"I've picked out the kids names already. Marco if it's a boy and Marca if it's a girl."

Tig quirks a brow.

"Marca?"

"Yeah, I'm not a fan of Marsha."

"You're fucking hopeless, you know that?"

"You love me," I say.

"Yeah, about as much as I love paying taxes. Come on, pay the man or you'll be late for traffic court."

ANTONIA

I'M GOING TO KILL MARCO when I get home for sending me another edible fruit arrangement. Don't get me wrong, it was very thoughtful and if I didn't have to haul it on the subway on my way to traffic court to fight the tickets he issued me the day we met, I might've rewarded him with a blow job.

Now, I'm sitting here, holding this ridiculous thing on my lap, waiting for the judge to call my name. At least I won't be here long. Back in the day, you used to be able to call a cop and have him pull the tickets, but because everything is electronic, Marco's hands were tied. The only way for me to get out of the tickets is for him not to show.

"Antonia DeLuca?"

"Here!"

Maneuvering the arrangement in my arms, I jump to my feet. The guard gives me a weird look, but I flash him a smile and offer him a strawberry.

Hey, it worked with Judy.

I step inside the courtroom and the smile falls from my face—the fruit falls too.

All over the damn courtroom.

"What are you doing here?" I ask Marco.

"I'm the officer who gave you those tickets. It's my job to be here."

If there wasn't a judge sitting as a witness I might—wait, where's the judge? My eyes dart around and I realize it's just me and Marco in the room.

Suddenly, he drops down on one knee in front of me and my heart—the organ I once deemed as treacherous, hammers in my chest. As luck would have it, my heart didn't betray me after all. It led me to the man of my dreams. The man I want to spend the rest of my life with.

"Antonia DeLuca—"

"Yes!" I blurt.

"What are you saying yes to? I didn't ask you anything."

Oh, right.

I should probably let him do that.

Smiling at me, he reaches into his pocket and pulls out a small velvet box.

"Three months ago, you blew a light and I pulled you over. You took off your helmet, shook out your hair and our eyes connected. I didn't realize I was staring at my future wife for the first time and I wrote you three tickets. One for speeding, another for blowing the light, and a third for failing to produce your insurance card."

"I remember."

He laughs.

"The thing about tickets though, is they are only valid if all the information on them is correct and there seems to be a discrepancy in your last name."

"Is that so?"

"Yeah, they should read Pirelli."

"It does have a nice ring to it," I whisper hoarsely.

"Speaking of rings…"

He flips open the box and turns it around. Nestled in the lush velvet is the most perfect engagement ring. My eyes fill with tears as they meet his and he takes my hand in his.

"Marry me, take my name, and give me the honor of loving you for the rest of my life."

"Yes, a million times yes!" I exclaim, pulling him to his feet. My lips collide with his and I wrap my arms around his neck. I never dreamed I'd be the girl who got the happy ending. After all, I'm the daughter of a criminal and he's a cop. We come from two different worlds, but somehow, we abolished the line drawn between us. We found love. We built trust. He took care of me and now, I get to take care of him for the rest of our lives.

Dear Anonymous,

First, let me start by apologizing for the delayed response. Your story sounds an awful lot like something a friend of mine is going through. She hasn't reached out to me and I suppose that's because I'm her boss and the cop she's dating happens to be a friend of mine as well. But I'll tell you exactly what I would tell her, not every guy is an asshole. The right man is out there, and he might not necessarily be your usual type or what you pictured for yourself, but you should still give him a chance. As for your dad, don't let his paranoia dictate the course of your life. Follow your heart.

It just might surprise you and who knows, it may even lead you to love of your life.

-Ida

P.S. Marco isn't a crooked cop

P.S.S. Answer your phone!

P.S.S.S. Antonia! You're fired.

P.S.S.S.S. (Is that even a thing) I was just kidding. You're not fired, but please answer your phone.

Want to keep up with all of the new releases in Vi Keeland and Penelope Ward's Cocky Hero Club world? Make sure you sign up for the official Cocky Hero Club newsletter for all the latest on our upcoming books:

https://www.subscribepage.com/CockyHeroClub

Check out other books in the Cocky Hero Club series:
http://www.cockyheroclub.com

ALSO BY
JANINE INFANTE BOSCO

THE TEMPTED SERIES:

Illicit Temptations

Forbidden Temptations

Uncontrollable Temptations

Reckless Temptations

Lethal Temptations

Eternal Temptations

THE NOMAD SERIES:

Drifter

Wanderer

Roamer

Loner

SATAN'S KNIGHTS TRANSITION OF POWER SERIES:

From the Ruins

The Devil Don't Sleep

Riding the Edge

Parrish

ABOUT
JANINE INFANTE BOSCO

Janine Infante Bosco lives in New York City and is an International Bestselling Author. When she was thirteen, she began to write her own stories and her passion for writing took off as the years went on. At eighteen, she even wrote a full screenplay with dreams of one day becoming a member of the Screen Actors Guild.

Janine writes emotionally charged novels with an emphasis on family bonds, strong willed female characters, and alpha male men who will do anything for the women they love. She loves to interact with fans and fellow avid romance readers like herself.

When she isn't writing, she is busy planning the Tempted & Tantalizing Author Event, an annual book signing in her hometown of Staten Island, New York. She also recently started a mystery box subscription services that caters to bad boy characters and the various authors who write them.

She is proud of her success as an author and the friend-ships she's made in the book community but her greatest accomplishment to date would be her two sons Joseph and Paul.

www.janineinfantebosco.com